All That Rises

A Post-Apocalyptic EMP Survival Thriller

JACK HUNT

DIRECT RESPONSE PUBLISHING

ISBN: 9781702604352

Also By Jack Hunt

The Renegades
The Renegades 2: Aftermath
The Renegades 3: Fortress
The Renegades 4: Colony
The Renegades 5: United
Mavericks: Hunters Moon
Killing Time
State of Panic
State of Shock
State of Decay
Defiant
Phobia
Anxiety
Strain
Blackout
Darkest Hour
Final Impact
And Many More…

Dedication

For my family.

Prologue

It was a painful sight.

Beth Sullivan stood in the warm sunroom observing from afar the interaction between Landon and Sara who'd stepped outside for privacy. Although she could have walked away and given them space, how could she? For seven months her instincts had been to stay close. She briefly cast a sideways glance at the stranger who'd only minutes earlier been lip-locked with Sara. He shifted from one foot to the next, red-faced and uncomfortable. Did he feel the same way? Though Landon had mentioned marriage troubles, she got a sense that it was minor, nothing more than the kind of ordeal that every couple faced. Still, seven months was a long time to be apart.

"Dad?" a voice said from behind her. Beth turned to see an emo looking kid, similar in age to her, and to his left some thin guy in an army jacket eying her with a smirk.

"You must be Max," she said. He acknowledged her with a nod. "Your dad mentioned you."

His brow furrowed. "Sorry. Who are you?"

"Oh, um, Beth," she said, extending a hand. "A friend of your father's." As he reached to shake it the other kid darted in front of him and took his place.

"Hellooo sweetheart. Aren't you a breath of fresh air. I'm Eddie. Eddie Raymond but you can call me..." He took a deep breath as if struggling to summon the words. "Well, whatever you like."

He flashed his pearly whites.

"I suggest douche bag." Max peered over his shoulder with a grin to which Eddie reacted by nudging him lightly in the gut, never taking his eyes off Beth for even a second.

"Ah… don't listen to him," he said waving his hand. "He's just sour. I was only telling Max yesterday that this town was in dire need of a pretty face. Wasn't I, Max?"

Beth pried her hand from Eddie's grip. Unimpressed, she raised an eyebrow and turned away to make it clear she wasn't interested. Max took a few steps toward the door that led out into the yard and the stranger stepped in front of him. "Uh, Max, you might want to give them a moment."

They couldn't hear the conversation outside but it was clearly not going well.

Max motioned with a finger. "Jake, that's my..."

Finally a name.

"Max, I know, but—"

As Max went to step by him, Jake placed a hand on his shoulder. His timing couldn't have been better. Sara let out a gut wrenching scream, similar to Dakota when she found her dead son. Heads swiveled. Sara pounded on Landon's chest before her legs buckled and she collapsed into his arms.

"Mom!" Max darted around Jake and had made it halfway between the house and his parents when Landon extended a hand of caution. A few words were exchanged, then Max staggered back, shaking his head before he turned and sprinted away without greeting his father. Beth squeezed her eyes shut, feeling the weight of the moment, knowing full well that Landon had just delivered the devastating news of Ellie's demise.

Near her knees, Grizzly whined as if sensing Landon's pain. "Come on, boy," she said lowering her head and turning to walk out.

Over the months of hiking the Appalachian Trail, they'd talked about how he would deliver the news if his family was still alive, but no amount of discussing could have prepared them for that.

Everyone in the house had heard the scream as several faces filled the hallway. Dakota emerged from the kitchen and met Beth on the way back. One glance, that was all it took. She didn't need to say anything as Landon had already given her the heads-up prior to arrival.

Beth took a seat at the kitchen table as others hurried to see what all the commotion was about. Although Landon had been hopeful about the coming days, and she wanted to believe there was a future for them, would others see it that way?

Chapter 1

Two days later

Mick Bennington hated to be associated with government, as they'd never done him any favors, but his hatred for Sam Daniels ran far deeper. Colonel Lukeman led him into the tent of FEMA rep David Harris. The spindly looking man clothed in a gray suit and red tie looked out of place among the military and survivors. His back was turned when they entered. He was staring at a map of the three counties. Harris reached up and inserted a red pin into the A-frame and wound a piece of twine around it and joined it with the location that represented the camp.

"Sir," Lukeman said.

Harris turned. "Ah. Colonel. And...?"

"Bennington, sir. Mick Bennington."

"Right. The man who says he can turn things around."
He chuckled as if he didn't buy it. "I sure hope so." He
motioned with a hand to a seat. "Please, take a load off."

The colonel left them alone. The vinyl-coated nylon
flooring crunched beneath his boots as he crossed the
room and sat down. The tent was far more unpretentious
than he expected. He'd heard rumors circulating that
Harris was living the good life while the rest of them were
in squalor. From what he could tell it was far from good.

"Coffee?" Harris asked as he poured from a thermos
into a plastic cup. Steam swirled above. Bennington gave
a nod.

It had been a long time since the massacre in Castine
and yet not a single day had passed that he hadn't
thought about how he could avenge the deaths of those
closest to him. He would have dealt with Sam by now
had most of his men not been wiped out, and had militia
not taken up guard in the town of Castine. That had
certainly thrown a wrench in the works and slowed things
down but it hadn't deterred him from his goal of

punishing Sam, and those who stood with him.

Harris handed him a cup and took a seat behind a desk. "So. I apologize that we haven't managed to speak sooner but my hands have been full."

"Trying your way?" Bennington asked as he took a sip of his drink.

Harris stared back and smiled. "You could say that." He lifted his eyes. "Castine has been more than a thorn in my side. I thought my offer was reasonable and Teresa thought your men could handle things. Perhaps that's why I'm a little hesitant to hear from you."

"What happened in Castine was out of my control. I didn't expect militia to assist."

"And yet here we are," Harris said, taking another sip of his coffee and making Bennington feel like a fool. "So, what great plan do you have that avoids more bloodshed? Because as it stands I can't afford to lose more soldiers."

Bennington shifted in his seat. "First, answer one question. Why don't you just ignore them?"

Harris smiled. "It would be easy to ignore them except

what occurred in Castine and Belfast has inspired other towns to resist and we can't afford to lose more." He swiveled in his seat and pointed to the map. "You see all those red pins. Those are the towns along the coast that are working with us. The blue pins are the ones that have cut ties and are refusing to assist. A month ago all of them were red barring Belfast and Castine." He turned back to him. "As you can see, things have changed. Some might say why bother? It's just a few towns. It's not as simple as that. I have a job to do here. We are limited both in manpower and where we receive resources. Initially we had enough but as time has passed and more people have come into the camp, we are faced with a dilemma. Do we turn people away or find new ways of feeding them?" He paused as if expecting Bennington to provide an answer. He didn't, so he continued. "If I force the people of this camp to help, we will be playing into the propaganda that is spreading that says we are labor camps." He reached over and took a stack of paper and tossed it in front of Bennington. He glanced at it. Sure enough, it was telling communities to cease fishing or providing any supplies to FEMA because they were running labor camps. "And you can tell from your stay that is simply not true. And if we take what we need by force, we are again villainized. Either people agree to help us or we must enforce martial law. So… as you can see, Mr. Bennington, I am in the unfortunate position of deciding what to do next. My priority are those people out there. However, until we put a stop to the militia, my hands are tied."

Bennington snorted. "And I thought you were just being dicks. You really are trying to help, aren't you?"

Harris set his coffee down on the table in front of him. "What other reason would we be here?"

"People in town think you are on a power trip. Even those in the camp think you are hoarding supplies for yourself."

Harris glanced out. "I expect they do."

Bennington sighed. "I can help but I want something in return."

"Name it."

"Full cooperation from your soldiers. What I say goes."

"I can't afford to lose more soldiers."

"You won't. They would only be used as a distraction."

"A distraction?"

Bennington nodded.

Harris ran a hand over his face. "I will run it by the colonel."

"No need. He would work under me."

Harris snorted. "And you think I am on a power trip."

Bennington leaned forward in his seat. "Look, man. It's no skin off my nose. I can walk out of here and go right back to what I was doing. Except what you are doing isn't working. If it was, we wouldn't be having this conversation. I've been a resident of Castine since I was a kid. I know that place like the back of my hand. Sure, things went south the first time around but that was because we were ambushed. We had no idea that would happen. However, this time, I plan on giving them some of their own medicine."

"Ambushing them?"

"No, something far better."

He studied Harris' face. He was intrigued.

"So…? Don't keep me in suspense."

Bennington leaned back in his seat. "We hamstring them."

Harris frowned. "Hamstring?"

"In days of old it was done to prevent horses from being used in warfare. Right now, Castine and Belfast's horses are the militia. Take them out of the agenda and you are left with but a few scared individuals. Ordinary folk. The same ones we managed to overpower."

"And the same ones who overpowered you."

Bennington shook his head and set his cup down. "Look, I'm gonna be blunt because you're starting to piss me off. You either want my help or you don't. But if you do, I would recommend being careful what you say next."

There was a long pause.

He waved his hand. "Go ahead. Continue," Harris replied.

A moment of hesitation and then he spoke. "We sabotage their efforts. A house divided will not stand," he said. "Right now the people think the militia are heroes. Modern-day outlaws. Like Robin Hood and his merry men. Taking from you and giving back to the people. So we must change that perception. Create a new story in the minds of locals. One that paints them in a different light."

Harris ran a hand over his jaw. "Create dissension?"

"Exactly," Bennington replied, jabbing his finger at him. "Going in guns blazing hasn't got you anywhere. First, you haven't managed to breach their checkpoints without coming under heavy fire and you've lost men. Additionally, sneaking in via the bay with a large group seeking to ambush them will only lead to more bloodshed and incite them to bump up security. So we take a different approach."

Harris cocked his head. "What do you have in mind?"

"It's been over a month since the last attack, correct?"

Harris nodded again.

"A small group will head in via the water. Leave it to us."

"Leave what to you?"

"The less I say the better," he said looking around. "You never know who might be listening. All I ask is that when we do it, you send some of the soldiers to the north end of the town. They'll expect an ambush but there's not enough of them to cover all of Castine. We'll enter and take it from there."

"You're going in?"

He gave a nod.

"Don't you think that's a little stupid since everyone knows you?"

"We don't plan on staying, Harris. Trust me. What I'm about to do will turn this around. And if we play this right, you won't have to waste a single bullet."

Harris got up and refilled his coffee. "I don't know. The last time I trusted you, you let me down."

"Well, do you have a better idea?"

"I want them out of there now. Not next week. Not

next month. Now."

"And you will but you need to approach this from a different angle unless you want more soldiers to die."

Bennington knew he had him by the balls. He wouldn't have gone to him if he thought he could pull it off alone but for it to work it relied on having a distraction.

Harris took a sip of his coffee and stared at the map. Bennington could see he was contemplating it. "I won't risk any more men dying."

"And you won't need to. You need to trust me."

Harris snorted as he turned. "Trust is earned. And I'm afraid you're a long way off."

Bennington could see he wasn't getting anywhere. "Fine. I get it. You need proof that I'm capable. What if I bring you proof?"

"Like what?"

"Leave that to me." He got up knowing what he had to do. Bennington expected Harris to be skeptical after the way things had ended. But if he wanted proof he would bring it. And he knew exactly where to start.

* * *

Jake Parish sat in the sunroom that morning consuming his second cup of coffee. His nerves were on edge and rightly so. Neither he nor Sara had expected Landon to show. Sam had joined him for moral support. While he didn't agree with how things had played out, he understood the importance of ensuring that the infrastructure they had in place remained intact. If he could have avoided the conversation he would have, but to move forward this had to be dealt with in person. The door opened and Landon stepped in closing it behind him. Jake's stomach dropped as he rose to his feet. "I appreciate you coming."

Landon eyed him and gave a nod before ambling over and taking a seat. He'd shaven and was now wearing a fresh dark shirt, and jeans.

Sam gave a nod. "Landon."

"Sam. I thought we were meant to be alone?" he asked.

"Precautionary."

"I see."

Jake blew out his cheeks and shifted uncomfortably in front of a window. "Look. This is difficult. In Sara's defense, she thought you were dead, Landon. Hank told her that he'd seen a charter plane go into the bay. When you didn't come home, she…"

"I get it," he replied leaning forward and lighting a cigarette. Both of them stared at him.

"You started again?" Jake asked. Landon's eyes lifted, a frown formed. "It's just that Sara said you were trying to quit."

He smirked, and blew smoke in his direction as if he didn't care. "Perhaps you should get to the point of why you wanted to see me. Better still, maybe you could tell me why you are still here in my home."

"Landon," Sam said. "As much as this is your home. The town is using it."

"With whose permission?"

"Sara's," Sam replied. "Without her help I'm sure many more would be dead." He took a deep breath. "A lot has happened since you've been gone. The only way we've managed to survive this long is by working together. That's why I'm here. We need to have each other's backs."

"Do we?" Landon asked in a manner which made it clear that he didn't believe that, even though it was the reason they had survived so far. He shrugged. "So... Sara's opened up the home. That doesn't mean you need to stay," he said, looking at Jake.

"Actually he does," Sam added. "His garage and home were destroyed not long after Bennington was put in charge."

"Bennington. Mick Bennington?"

Sam gave a nod.

"Huh. Things must have been bad."

Sam nodded. "There's been a lot of bloodshed. I don't know how much Sara has told you but—"

"She hasn't told me anything. She's locked herself in her room for the past two days, which is another reason why I think you should all leave."

"I beg to differ," Jake said. "She needs us."

"No. She needs her family."

"We've been that family," Jake said. "Rita, Janice, Tess, Sam, Carl and the others."

Landon raised a finger. "I appreciate that but now it's time to move on. Things change."

Sam leaned forward, his hands clasped together. "Landon."

"Sam. Look. I don't know you very well. In fact, where is Carl?"

"Carl went on a run outside of Castine with a few of the militia. Collection of supplies."

Landon blew smoke out the corner of his mouth. "Well. As much as I appreciate you showing up here today, let's make something clear. Sara. Max. They're my family. This is my home. And regardless of what decisions were made before. I'm telling you. It's time to leave."

"They're staying," Sara said from off to his right. Neither one of them had heard her enter. "I invited them and they're staying."

"But Sara—"

"I'm not sending them away." She looked over at Jake.

Landon looked back at Jake. It was clear she had feelings for him. Had he set this up? Already spoken with Sara? He felt ambushed, pushed into a corner. Was he meant to be okay with this arrangement? Landon rose to his feet. "You know. I think we are done here. You wanna stay. Stay. But that doesn't mean I have to." He turned to leave.

"Landon," Jake said. "Come on, man. You've just returned. Look, if it's that much of a problem I'll go."

Landon ignored him. What did he expect him to say? Stay? He could see how this was going to be turned around to make him look like the bad guy. It was unreal. When he reached the door he expected Sara to stop him, say something, but she didn't. She simply sidestepped and lowered her head. He stopped beside her. "I'll be at your mother's. When Max returns, let him know where I am."

He continued walking until Sara said over her shoulder, "She's dead."

Landon stopped in his tracks and looked back. He wanted to say something but what could be said? "I..." He trailed off unable to process everything that had happened. Landon walked down the hallway until he reached the kitchen where Beth and Dakota were. "I'm taking my bag and heading to my mother-in-law's. You are welcome to stay or come with me."

"You should know me better than that," Beth said rising along with Dakota. As they stepped out into the hallway he looked back at Sara who watched them leave. He didn't want it to come to this, nor did he want to feel like a stranger in his own home, but that's how he felt. And from the lack of support from Sara he assumed she didn't want him there either.

Chapter 2

Something was wrong. On a secluded farm, five miles west of Ellsworth, Carl Madden dismounted from his horse, a look of concern spreading. The home belonged to Sheriff Wilson. Within the first month after the blackout he'd wisely made a point to visit Ellsworth Ammo Company to collect a cache of ammunition. It was back then that he realized Wilson knew more about the event than he did, as in years gone by they'd had blackouts and never once was he concerned about running out of ammunition.

The small family-run business operated out of a small factory just on the outskirts of Ellsworth. Wilson had taken Carl with him and purchased boxes upon boxes of ammo. It was the same company that provided law enforcement with theirs and so Carl assumed it was for the department. It wasn't.

In the months after the blackout and before Teresa

pulled that stunt of having their badges taken, he and Sam had taken several trips out to Wilson's farm to collect more ammo. Today was meant to be no different.

"He knows you're coming?" Lee Ferguson asked

"Oh, yeah, we go way back."

"And yet he agreed to let Teresa take your badge."

"Small-town politics. He wouldn't have done it had FEMA not applied pressure. Me and Wilson are like this," he said raising up two fingers and crossing them.

Lee instructed two of his guys to watch their six while they entered the two-story clapboard home. Parked outside was a police SUV, and nearby was a horse tied up. Seven months into the blackout, he'd learned that Wilson had resigned from his position and those in the county jail had been transported to the FEMA camp.

"Wilson!" Carl said hopping up onto the creaky porch and opening the storm door. A fine layer of dust was on the porch rocker as if it hadn't been used in a while. He tried the handle but it was locked. Carl peered in but it was hard to see through the thin drapes. He rapped the door a few times with his knuckles then looked back at Lee. "He's probably napping."

Only a week earlier, he and Sam had paid Wilson a visit to discuss the change of power in Castine and to request supplies. At first he'd kicked up a fuss and said that they were no longer cops and the ammo was the property of Hancock County Sheriff Department. Sam worked his magic on him by offering additional fish in return and Wilson soon agreed to provide them with whatever they needed. It wasn't like he needed much. There was only him since his wife of thirty-two years had passed away five years earlier from breast cancer.

"Wilson. You sleeping? Get up. It's Carl."

He made his way around and looked through another window before trying the rear door. Again it was locked. He groaned. He didn't want to come all this way for nothing. Everything was stored in the basement under the floorboards just in case he encountered a home invasion.

"So?" Lee asked.

Carl shrugged. "I'll break a window," he said moving

toward the closest one.

"No, there's a window open on the second floor," Lee said stepping back and pointing. Carl stepped off the porch and cupped a hand over his eyes to block the glare of sunlight. Sure enough one window was slightly cracked open. The drapes were gently blowing in the morning breeze.

"All right, give me a boost," he said getting near the porch. Lee interlinked his fingers and thrust Carl upward. He latched on to the roof and clambered up until he made it to the window. Carl looked over his shoulder across the farm. A warm breeze blew against his face. It was so peaceful. No vehicles. Just rolling fields of tall grass surrounded by woodland. He pushed up the window and climbed inside dropping to the floor. "Hey, Wilson. It's me, Carl. Don't you go shooting me," he said wanting to make sure he didn't spook him. "I know we weren't meant to be up here for another few weeks but we've plowed through that cache." He stepped into the hallway and looked into Wilson's bedroom. The covers were pulled back. He strolled down the landing and stairs expecting to find him in the living room. Sure enough, there he was. Bottle of whiskey on the floor nearby. Carl scooped it up and placed it on the table. "You old dog. I told you that..." As he came around his eyes widened and he went for his gun. Wilson was in his recliner chair but he wasn't alive. His throat had been slit from ear to ear. His shirt was drenched in blood. It wasn't dry which meant it had happened less than an hour, maybe even thirty minutes ago. Fear shot through him as he hurried for the front door and let Lee in. "He's dead."

"What?"

He didn't repeat himself but immediately made a beeline for the basement. The door was ajar. Carl bounded down the steps taking two at a time. He'd turned on his flashlight and the light bounced off the walls.

Sure enough his fears were confirmed. The floorboards had been taken up and the boxes of ammo were gone. "Shit!" Then it dawned on him. Whoever had done this had gone to a lot of trouble to lock the doors. Why would you do that? They had obviously exited via the window but why?

As he turned to head back upstairs an eruption of gunfire echoed. Carl bounded up the stairs in time to see Lee kick the front door shut. "We're under attack."

"No shit," he replied as rounds riddled the walls and windows sending shards of glass and drywall dust everywhere. Carl stayed low and inched his way over to Lee. "How many?"

"At least four. They took out Holman and Sommers."

Carl made his way into the living room and sidled up beside the window and looked out. He saw six guys fanning out, military, reserves by the looks of it. Lee returned fire sending them rushing for cover. Carl was packing a Winchester rifle and a Beretta 92. He stuck the rifle out the window and managed to hit one of them in the leg taking him down. Lee hurried over. "Please tell me this was not for nothing."

"The ammo is gone."

"Shit!" Lee said. "We need to get out of here."

He hurried toward the rear only to be driven back by more gunfire. "They've got the place surrounded."

They stayed low and positioned themselves so that Lee had the rear entrance in sight, and Carl could see anyone approaching the main door. Right then a familiar voice came over a megaphone.

"There's no way out. You might as well come on out. No one else will get hurt."

"Bennington," Carl muttered as he sneaked a peek.

"Come on out!"

"You've stepped over the line, Bennington," Carl hollered.

"Like you did when you cut down your own people in cold blood?"

"The same people that locked us up," Carl replied.

"That was on me not them," Bennington replied.

"You, them. They were in the same bed as you."

"We never killed anyone. You've brought this on yourselves," Bennington said. "Now you've forced my hand."

Carl checked how much ammo he had left. His rifle was empty but he had the handgun. "Lee. How much ammo you got?"

"Enough," he said inching out and taking another look down the hallway.

"Come on, Carl. You know this only ends one way. You either walk out and come back to the camp with us or we leave you out here."

Carl ran a hand over his face. "That bastard must have been watching us."

Carl had tried to convince Wilson to let them take the remaining ammo back to Castine the last time they were out, but Wilson wouldn't let them. In his mind, he paid for it, he owned it. But that was bullshit. It was covered by the department.

"We walk out of here, we are screwed," Lee replied.

He nodded. He knew Bennington was playing with them. "I'm going high. See how many there are," Carl said, running at a crouch toward the staircase. He had to pass in front of the main door. His silhouette prompted another flurry of rounds, drilling the door so hard that it burst open. He hurried up the stairs and made his way to the back bedroom with the open window. No sooner had he reached the doorway than he saw one of Bennington's men climbing in. He opened fire, taking him out, and then fired two more shots at a second man who was behind him. The rounds struck him in the chest sending him off the roof.

That only caused another burst of gunfire sending glass everywhere.

"You still with me, Carl?" Lee yelled.

"In the flesh," he replied. He darted into another room and tried to get a better idea of how many there were and where they were positioned. They were everywhere. There had to have been at least ten of them. He took a few steps back and sank down onto the floor. A gut-wrenching feeling came over him, a sense that he wasn't getting out of this alive. He had no family. No wife. Besides Sam there would be no one to miss him. As strange as it seemed, he began to think about all his life choices. Every decision he'd made that had led up to this. *Think. Think. You're a cop for God's sake. You once knew how to handle this kind of situation.* But that was back when he had a radio, dispatch, an entire department ready at his beck and call.

Now they were alone.

A loud bang echoed and multiple rounds erupted.

He didn't need to see it to know what had happened. They'd stormed the house. He wanted to call out to Lee but he expected he was dead by now. Instead, he shifted up a window and slipped out, made his way over the ridge and tried to find a way down where there weren't soldiers. But they were on every side.

Straddling the roof he was about to go back into the house when he saw Bennington walking backwards looking up at him. "Don't make me bring you down," he said. Right then two men dragged Lee out. He was still alive but had been shot up pretty bad. Carl wasn't the type to grovel so he fell back on the only thing he had, communication. The one skill the police had taught him. Most situations could be deescalated through communicating. Was this any different?

He slipped down the roof slowly. A soldier was waiting for him, beckoning him to toss his weapon down and come back inside. A moment of indecision and then he complied. The moment he entered the window, he was thrown to the ground and beaten with rifle butts before being dragged outside and tossed in front of Bennington.

Bennington had this smug look on his face as he crouched down and ran a hand over his hair like he was petting a dog. "There, there, deputy. It's going to be okay." Without missing a beat, he turned and fired a round into Lee's skull, killing him instantly. He then brought the gun up to Carl's head. "I told Sam I would kill him and I'm a man of my word."

"What did you expect to happen?" Carl asked.

"Respect. The same kind I gave to you both."

Carl frowned. "Respect? Beating an officer of the law?"

"He gave me no option. We didn't pull the trigger

first."

"So that makes it okay now?"

"Survival."

Carl snorted then spat blood onto the ground near Bennington's boot. "If you're gonna kill me, just get it over with, I'm tired of listening to your bullshit."

"Oh, I'm not going to kill you, Carl. Not yet. You're going to send a message to Sam."

"Yeah, why… you a secret admirer?"

Bennington chuckled as he put his gun away and stepped back. He motioned to those around him and smiled as multiple soldiers stepped in and began to unleash the worst beating he'd ever received. Boots struck him in the face, gun butts cracked his ribs and someone twisted his foot until he heard his bones break. Carl screamed in agony. All the while Bennington looked on, relishing the moment.

* * *

Ray Ferguson rolled off Teresa's naked body and reached for a pack of smokes on the table beside the bed.

She slung an arm around his waist and he raked his fingers through her hair before offering a cigarette. He lit the end and she got up and inhaled deeply as she wandered into the bathroom. "You know, we need to keep this between you and me," she said. "I can't have anyone knowing about this."

"Suits me fine," he said, inhaling hard.

She stuck her head out of the bathroom. "It's nothing personal but appearances are everything and I can't have people thinking I'm just using you to remain here in Castine."

"Are you?"

"What?"

"Using me."

"Of course." She chuckled.

"Now I feel cheap," he replied, before laughing. He didn't give two shits. It was a warm bed and finding a good woman to ease his stress was just what he needed. After they'd taken back Castine and watched the military leave, Ray had been quick to set up checkpoints and make sure that the people were on board with helping, that included the town manager. One look and he knew the relationship between them was going to be fun. Many in the town objected and villainized her, saying she was sleeping with Harris, and that's why Bennington had been put in charge. Others said she was just in it for the additional supplies. Whatever her reasons were, he didn't care. She was good in bed and her insight into what Harris was up to was something he couldn't pass up. If anyone was using anyone, it was him.

"So you said Harris told you that he was supposed to be receiving additional support from the south?"

"That's right. Another fifty men."

"And when are they arriving?"

"Today or tomorrow. Whether they do or not is to be seen but just a heads-up, you might not want to be around when they show." She continued rattling on about how Harris was planning on making an example of Castine, killing the militia and hanging their bodies in public as a message to everyone. He stopped listening; his mind switched to his brother.

Ray sucked on the cigarette as he got up and went over to the window.

"If they show, we'll be ready," he replied.

Teresa came up behind him and wrapped her arms around his waist. "What about me?"

"What about you?" he said turning into her.

"The people of this town don't like me."

"Sure they do."

"No, they endure me. There is a big difference."

"Does it matter?"

"Like I told you. Appearances matter. That's why I have an idea. I want you to make it known that this news about Harris came from me. Restore their faith in my ability to…"

"Teresa. I learned a long time ago that people don't care what comes out of your mouth. They look at your actions. You want respect, admiration, people looking up to you, then you've got to do something for them. That means sacrifice. Are you willing to sacrifice for others?"

She pulled away. "You know I'm taking a big risk. I could quite easily inform Harris of…"

Before she could finish he grabbed her by the wrist and held it tightly. "You can use me. But if I learn you have jeopardized the safety of my men. You won't need to worry about Harris, I will put a bullet in your head myself. We clear?"

She sneered as she struggled in his grasp.

"You're hurting me."

"Are we clear?" he bellowed.

She gritted her teeth. "Crystal."

Right then there was a knock at the door. He released her and looked out the window. Down below Max was pacing. "Great, what's he want?" he muttered.

"Who is it?" Teresa asked.

"Sara's son. Max," Ray said slipping into his jeans.

"How does he know you're here?"

"The same way all my guys know where I am. I told them."

"What?!" she stammered. "But I specifically told you."

He didn't stick around to listen to her moaning. He rolled his eyes as he walked out, doing his shirt up on the way down.

Chapter 3

Landon shouldered the door on his mother-in-law's three-bedroom home and entered with a heavy heart. He stepped out of the way and beckoned the other two in. The familiar smell of potpourri in bowls brought back a flood of memories: birthdays, Thanksgiving, Christmas. Although her parents weren't exactly thrilled with Sara marrying Landon because of his line of work, they embraced him as a son-in-law and were always cordial with him.

Rita had told him before they left that Sara had buried Cathy in a small plot at the back of the home. He made his way to the rear of the house, and saw a cross sticking out of the earth. He dropped his bag on the kitchen table which was covered with mail, magazines and a to-do list dated a few days before Christmas. Not saying a word to Beth or Dakota he strolled out to pay his respects.

A warm breeze blew against his skin as he strolled

across the grass, past a large fountain no longer pumping out water. It was now covered in leaves from winter. He could almost hear their voices, and the sound of meat sizzling on the BBQ from days gone by. So many memories — now just fleeting, vague images that he would soon forget. Not far from the garden shed was a small mound of earth surrounded by small pebbles. Dead flowers were scattered over the top. He bent down and brushed them away and picked a few wildflowers from the flower bed nearby and replaced them.

Landon crouched in silence before muttering a few words under his breath as Beth sidled up beside him. "You okay?"

He gave a nod.

"Look, you didn't have to come. You could have stayed at the Manor," he said.

"Without you? I think you know me better than that." He smiled. "You wanna talk about it?"

He hadn't said anything since leaving. The short journey from the Manor to the north end of Castine was filled with silence. Beth and Dakota kind of knew his return wouldn't be easy and their time on the AT had taught them that sometimes it was better to say nothing than to force an issue.

He shrugged. "What was I meant to do? Stay?"

"I probably would have done the same thing," she said.

He rolled a pebble in his hand. "I'm not saying we won't go back but I just need some time to think and with him there, well…" He looked up at Beth. He didn't see an eighteen-year-old girl but someone who was wise beyond her years.

"Sara didn't stop you?" She asked.

"Sara doesn't want to speak to me. She blames me for Ellie's death."

"But that was out of your control. The power went out."

"I encouraged her to come along with me."

Beth studied him. "She could have died crossing the road."

"No, I know. She's in pain and wants someone to

blame and right now that's me."

Beth nodded. "I don't envy your position. What about Max?"

"I tried to talk to him over the last few days but he's not been around. Rita said he ducks in late at night and is up before the crack of dawn. She says he's hanging out with the militia group here in town. Which reminds me, that's another thing I need to deal with."

"The militia?"

"His involvement. I'm not having him caught up in it."

"Sounds like he already is." She paused. "Word of advice, Landon. Go easy on him. Until you know what he's been through, you're liable to just get a reaction out of him. If you like, I could speak to him."

"You?"

She cracked a smile. "Why not? He's the same age as me. Probably more inclined to listen to me than to—"

"Me?"

"I was going to say an adult but… yeah."

Landon shook his head. "I can't ask you to do that, I need to handle it."

"And you will but all in good time, right? Let me smooth things out a little, help him to understand what you've just been through."

Landon pulled a face. "I dunno, Beth."

"Landon. Let me take some of the weight. You've done it for me. It's the least I can do." He nodded and thanked her. She thumbed over her shoulder. "Well, I guess we should get settled in."

Beth strolled into the house with Grizzly in her shadow. He remained there for a few minutes more, taking a moment to feel the grief and loss before rising.

* * *

Max knocked on the door for a fourth time. He knew he was in there and he wasn't leaving until he spoke with him. "Yeah, yeah, I'm coming. Hold your horses." The door swung open and Ray stepped out tucking his shirt into his pants. His zipper was still down and his hair was a mess. "Kid, this better be important."

"I'll do it," Max said.

"What?"

"Go into the camp."

Ray looked over his shoulder and saw Teresa. He reached for the handle and closed the door, then put a hand around Max's shoulder and led him away. Although he was screwing her, the less she knew about what he had in mind the better. After multiple attacks on Castine and several deaths, they'd had to rethink their strategy. Lee had come up with an idea to have a few of the men go into the camp under the ruse they were seeking shelter and provisions. Of course they would be wearing civilian clothing and the logic behind it was to get a feel for what was happening. Basically be a Trojan horse. Find ways to attack from inside the walls, learn more about what they were planning and so on.

Ray patted Max on the shoulder. "It was just an idea, kid. Nothing has been agreed upon."

"Well when you decide to move ahead, I'm your man."

"No."

"Why not? Is it my age?"

He chuckled. "Max, you have balls of steel. Hell, you put to shame several of our guys in our unit but it's not because of that. Bennington is working with them and after the stunt you pulled killing two of his guys, you're liable to get yourself strung up."

"That was a long time ago."

"That it was, but he hasn't forgotten. No. I'm not sending you in. Besides, your mother would go apeshit on me." He laughed as they strolled over to a bench that overlooked the bay. Teresa owned a huge lot that backed up to the bay and offered some incredible views. The salty air drifted in as Ray reached into his top pocket and took out a pack of smokes. He offered one to Max but he declined.

"Then what can I do?"

"Just stay available. You could help out at the checkpoints."

"I don't wanna stand around all day. I want a piece of

the action."

Ray lit the end. It glowed a bright orange and he sucked on the cigarette. "You got a death wish, kid?"

"I'm just tired of waiting around to become a victim."

Ray squinted as he blew gray smoke out the corner of his mouth. "I hear your old man is back in town. Heard he was gone for seven months. I would have thought you'd want to spend time with him."

"Well you thought wrong," Max said wiping his hands on his pants and tapping his foot. He'd consumed a crazy amount of caffeine that morning, so his nerves were on edge. "He didn't return with my sister."

There was a pause. "Oh. I see. I'm sorry. That's got to be hard."

Max shrugged. "Anyway, I just wanted to let you know that if you need someone to go in, or don't have enough people who are willing, I'll do it. To hell with Bennington. He can't exactly hang me in front of all those people."

"But he can punish you. No. You're not thinking

clearly, kid."

"Stop calling me kid. I'm not a kid. Okay?"

Ray blew out smoke and nodded. "You got it." He rose. "Look, I have to get back to…"

"Banging Teresa?"

"To what I was doing before that," he said. "And watch your mouth."

"You know what. Thanks for nothing. You are just like the rest of them. All they want to do is talk. I'm done with talking." He got up and Ray tried to stop him but Max took off.

"Max. You're not thinking clearly. C'mon. Let's talk about it."

As the words came out of his mouth, Max glared at him before vanishing around the corner of the house. If it wasn't for the fact that he reminded him of himself when he was a kid, or that he truly thought Max had the potential to be a good soldier, he wouldn't have given him the time of day or cared, but he did. He didn't want him getting hurt any more than his own men and in some ways he felt responsible.

* * *

Max knew where to find him. Nautilus Island had once again become his own private paradise. An isolated retreat away from the madness of a world without power. Eddie Raymond was dressed in Hawaiian shorts and smoking a fat doobie and bobbing around in the swimming pool on an inflatable chair when Max showed up looking red-faced and out of breath. "Maxy boy! The man of the hour. I was just thinking about you. Pull up a chair, enter my office and let's discuss business."

"Eddie, I don't have time for your crap. The cache of weapons, where did you put them?"

After the incident on Castine between militia and Bennington's group, they had gathered up an arsenal of weapons and ammo from the dead and were supposed to hand it over to Ray once it was over. He, however, having a fond love of business saw an opportunity in the making. Eddie opted to take a portion of the cache and bury it with the grand idea of trading it for... well... whatever the hell he could get.

"Oh I moved it."

"Why?"

"Well you know, security and whatnot. You never really know who's watching or listening."

Max palmed his forehead. "Man, your brilliance continues to amaze me. Where is it?"

"Ram Island."

"Are you kidding me?"

"No."

"Why would you take it there?"

"Why wouldn't I?"

"Uh because this island we're on is massive, and maybe because you could have left it over on Castine. Fuck, Eddie."

He sat up. "Why do you care anyway? You have a Walther P99."

"I need something more powerful."

"Well then you have come to the right man." He stuck his doobie in his mouth and paddled over to the edge, nearly falling into the water as he climbed out. "What have you got to barter with?"

"Barter?"

"Yeah, you think Hugh Hefner built his empire by giving away shit for free?"

"First, you're not Hugh Hefner. And second, half of that cache is mine."

"I buried it."

"I collected it."

"So did I."

Max raised a finger. "Eddie."

"Okay, okay!" He threw his hands up. "You push a hard bargain; I'll give you one rifle for free."

"Eddie!"

"Fuck." He stomped over to a pool chair and got back into some clothes all the while complaining. "How the hell am I meant to build my empire when you keep dipping your hand into my wealth?"

"Shut up and just get your shit together and let's go."

* * *

It didn't take long to reach the tiny island. The seven acres of land was south of Nautilus. It consisted of two islands joined together by a bar at low tide and was mostly used by those looking to picnic and observe wildlife. The bow of the boat bounced up onto the shore and Eddie jumped out to tie it off to a tree. "I still don't see why you don't wait for Ray," he said.

"Because they've lost interest. Everything has to go through meetings especially now that he's screwing Teresa."

"Come on, you're joking?"

"You didn't know?" Max asked. He climbed onto a boulder and made his way up to the tree line.

"No. Gross! I know we're in desperate times but I wouldn't go near that with a barge pole. Eeek." He snorted leading the way.

Max scanned the terrain. "Right, where did you leave it?"

"Not far from here," he said trudging through the thick foliage. There was nothing on the island except trees and underbrush. When he made it to the spot, both of them stared into a large hole in the ground that was empty. Eddie jabbed his finger at the hole. "No. No. I placed it all here." He looked around before catching the eye of Max, who was shaking his head.

"Why does this not surprise me?"

"Hey. I placed it here. No one saw me."

"Well obviously someone did. Great. Great. Now what am I supposed to do?"

Eddie stared back at him. "Well, you wait. Listen to Ray. Besides, you saw how things turned out the last time we got involved."

"Yeah, I was the catalyst to get shit rolling. And right now nothing is rolling."

"But we're alive, Max. That matters to me. Why don't we just go back to Nautilus, crack open a bottle of wine, smoke a few doobies and chill?"

"I'm done chilling," Max said charging off toward the boat. Eddie was quick to catch up.

"What's got up your ass?"

"Everything. My old man. My sister." He sighed.

"You never told me."

"You were there."

"No, I mean that it bothered you."

Max pitched sideways pulling a face. "Would you have cared?"

"Well no but hey… it's news, right?"

"Yeah, well…"

"So…" Eddie said as Max clambered into the boat and he untied the rope from the tree. "If he's returned, why are you looking to go all kamikaze?"

"I'm not. I'm just…" Max clenched his jaw and looked out across the bay. Eddie tossed the rope into the boat and climbed in.

"Look, you don't want to tell me, fine, but if you want my help, then…"

"She's dead. Okay. My sister is dead."

There was a long pause as Max began to row.

"Shit. That's heavy. Sorry, man."

"Yeah, well, now you know."

A herring gull wheeled overhead squawking. The gentle lapping of the water against the boat brought his mind back to the past. The numerous times he'd spent with his sister. Her laughter. Their jokes. Things that to others would have been meaningless but now meant so much more. He rowed in silence for another five minutes before Eddie piped up. "I know what it feels like."

"No you don't."

"I do."

"No. No you don't!" Max bellowed back, letting his grief get the better of him.

There was silence for a few minutes.

"Did I ever tell you about my older brother Richie?"

He shook his head.

"Died in a car crash when I was nine."

Max looked at him. "You never told me."

"Never asked."

Max studied him. "I thought it was just you."

Eddie shook his head. "Nope." He breathed in deeply. "Anyway. I know what it feels like, Max. You just want to run, hide, do anything dangerous just to feel alive."

"Well that's the thing, I don't want to be alive."

"Yeah, you do."

"No I don't."

Eddie smirked. "That hot chick that arrived with your father. I saw the way you eyed her."

"I didn't eye her."

"Please. You were all over her. If I hadn't intervened, you would have been drooling at the mouth."

Max laughed and Eddie leaned over and patted him on the arm. "See. You want to live. I mean unless you want me to sweep in there and scoop her up. And believe me, it would be my honor." He grinned. They both breathed in the salty air as they made their way back. Eddie continued to rattle on about where his cache had gone, and Max thought about the girl who'd arrived with his father. Eddie wasn't far wrong. Beth was something else. Beautiful. Definitely hot.

Chapter 4

Sara had never been an anxious person but since the blackout she'd found herself consuming more alcohol just to keep her calm. She'd taken to carrying a small portable flask of vodka and orange juice that she would swig when she felt her emotions getting the better of her. That afternoon was no exception. Not wishing for anyone to know, she had opted to take a walk in the woods at the back of the house where Landon had installed a small bench. It had been a quiet and special place they would go to when they needed time to think and talk. Nearby was a small brook that ran through the woods and flowed into a pond. Max often used it for fishing.

"I thought I would find you here," Jake said.

Startled, and concerned about what Jake would say, she tucked the flask beneath her jacket and turned. He came around. "You mind?" he asked gesturing to the bench.

"Go ahead."

He sighed as he sank down. "Quite a morning, eh?"

"You could say that."

They sat staring at the brook, watching the water flow over rocks and through the landscape. A cluster of birds broke away from a tree and Jake looked up. "You ever just wanted to be a bird and soar above it all? No pressures. No attachments. Just fly for miles and miles?"

She gave a strained smile. "Many times."

"Did he ever take you up?"

"Once. Scared the daylights out of me."

He rubbed his hands together. "I always wanted to fly. Never got around to it. Spent my entire life in Castine and never once ventured beyond Maine. Crazy, right?"

"Not really. I've only been to Florida, and Arizona. Life gets busy and it's expensive to travel."

He nodded. "Yeah." He inhaled deeply and turned toward her. "Sara. What happened between you and me. Um. I understand if you…"

"I don't regret it," she replied, glancing at him.

"Nor do I but…" He studied her face as if trying to gauge how she was feeling. "However, things will change now, right?" he asked.

She shrugged. "I don't know. I don't know anything." She tilted her head and looked up through the canopy of lush green leaves. "I just can't believe my girl is gone."

He reached for her hand and gave it a reassuring squeeze. She appreciated it yet at the same time couldn't help but feel different about him. On one hand she wanted to tell him to leave the house but on the other hand she didn't.

"What are you going to do?" Jake asked. "About Landon."

"Speak with him, I guess."

"And say what?"

She shook her head and looked down into her hands, rolling around the wedding ring that at one time meant so much to her but now had become foreign. "I don't know."

Jake nodded and looked away.

"I should move out. It's not right for me to stay."

"No. Stay."

He shook his head. "Landon was right. It's his home. If I came home after seven months away and walked in on my wife kissing another man, I'd be more than pissed. I'm surprised he didn't lynch me."

"That's not like him."

"No? You killed people. I'm sure he has. This whole event has changed us. I didn't think I could take another person's life but I have. Anyway that's why I came to see you today. I wanted to let you know that I'm moving out."

Her expression changed. Her mouth widened. "And if I don't want you to go?"

Jake smiled. "Look, Sara. The time we spent together was… well.. it meant a lot. It was good. Really good. And if I had my way I would spend the rest of my days with you but that's not reality. Reality is you are married and Landon is home now and whatever becomes of your marriage after this, that's for you both to decide. I don't want to get in the way. I would have never moved in on you had I known that he was still alive." He shook his head. "I mean, I didn't know whether he was dead or alive but... I guess I just wanted to be with you." He paused for a second. "I've always wanted to be with you."

She didn't know how to respond to that except to nod.

"Where will you go?" She asked.

"Sam said I could take the spare room in his place."

"He's going back?"

"With the way things are at the moment, FEMA staying away and whatnot, he thinks it's probably time we got back to some normality."

"Normality? But there's still no power."

"No power grid, yes, but I've been talking with Rodney Jennings about alternative forms of power. Wind and hydropower. It might take some time but if the community works together we may be able to get the lights back on again using a few of the ideas he has. I'm not sure it would power appliances but who knows. Rodney seems quite confident and after his little ice experiment, well, I think that would be something worthwhile to give my time to."

Sara frowned. "And what does Ray have to say about all this? Or Sam? What about the shifts that the community is involved with to protect residents?"

"It's been over a month since the last attack. Ray has every intention of having the community and his men continue to protect the area but we will eventually need to pick up from where we left off and focus on... well... life." He paused for a second. "And that means you and Landon having time to be a family." He paused for a second. "Sam said something about us heading out to Ellsworth because Carl hasn't returned. On the way out, I'll drop my stuff off at his place. I just wanted to let you know."

Her chin dropped.

"I'll still drop by from time to time. You know, to check in on you and Max. Make sure things are good. I'm not going anywhere but... Landon was right. And he has every right to be angry and want time with his family. I want to respect his wishes."

"And what about mine?" she asked turning toward him.

"You must have known he might one day return."

"Did you?"

He shook his head.

"But…"

She screwed up her face, closed her eyes, then nodded. Jake gave her hand one more squeeze before he went to pull away. As he did, she leaned over and kissed him. Somewhere inside she knew it was wrong but in that moment she wasn't thinking about Landon, the next day or what might happen, only what she felt for Jake. In their time together he had unearthed deep-seated feelings. Feelings she didn't even realize were there until recently. She parted from him and took a deep breath. Jake got up and told her he would see her tomorrow, at the town hall meeting. There was meant to be a big discussion about the recent attacks, shift work and farming which had taken priority over the recent months.

* * *

As Jake emerged from the tree line, Sam was coming out of the house. "Ah, there you are. You ready to go?"

He nodded. "I just have to grab my bags."

"Already loaded them on the horses."

"Huh, you're eager."

Sam turned and they walked side by side around the house to the horses. "He should have been back by now. I don't like it."

"Perhaps they decided to stay there the night."

Sam shook his head. "No. With everything that's happened, it's too risky."

"Well then, don't you think we should inform Ray?"

Sam never replied.

As they made their way over to the stable, Max and Eddie were coming up the driveway on their bikes. "Your mother is looking for you," Jake said. "She's out back."

"Where are you going?" Max asked.

Jake dipped his head slightly and told Sam to give him a minute. Sam disappeared into the stables while Jake approached Max. "I'm moving out. Staying at Sam's."

"Sam's going too?"

"Yeah. For a while. But I'll swing by."

Max pursed his lips. "This is because of my dad, isn't it?"

Jake gave a strained smile. "You should take some time to be with him."

"I don't have anything to say."

"Maybe you don't need to say anything. Just listen." He looked off toward the stables where Sam emerged with two horses. "He's staying at your grandmother's place."

"Why?"

"Talk to your mother. She'll explain." He placed a hand on his shoulder. "Stay out of trouble. Okay?" Max didn't reply. Eddie had the usual grin on his face. "I gotta go." Jake turned and joined Sam. He gave one last look at Max and the Manor before giving the horse a nudge. They guided the horses down the driveway and took off at a gallop heading north toward Sam's home.

"You really have bonded with him."

"Max? Yeah. He's a good kid. A little lost but his heart is in the right place."

"You're doing the right thing. If Sara decides to go her separate way then well, at least Landon can't say you didn't give them a chance."

"Now you change your tune," Jake replied.

"Hey, I don't want to leave the Manor any more than you do but if it keeps the peace that's all that matters to me. Besides, I have enough on my plate to worry about."

"Bennington, you mean?"

Sam gave a nod as they kept a steady pace. "Yeah. He's not the kind of man that will walk away. I know the community is eager to get back to regular living but until he's dealt with we have a dark cloud overshadowing us. It's just a matter of time before he shows his face and when he does I don't want to be caught off guard."

The town of Castine had changed a lot since the blackout. A lot of structures were in ruins from the fights between military and militia, but amid the disarray there was a spark of hope, a sense that people might be able to get back to their normal lives. And the strange part was Rodney Jennings had been instrumental in that. While he was useless when it came to shooting a gun, his mind was brilliant. It had been because of him that they had been able to keep fish fresh for longer with the ice he made using equal parts water and acetone. Of course they couldn't toss a chunk in a glass but for packing around items it was perfect.

The next thing on the agenda was delving into alternative forms of power. They already had a few portable wind turbines but they were looking to create more, enough to power battery banks that could store the power and then provide light to homes. And with so much water in the area from the bay, streams and rivers, they were already in the planning stage of finding a way to harness it to create hydroelectricity. All that was required was large volumes of falling water and to create that, they were considering building a dam. Rodney said he had it all figured out. He'd even shown Jake this large whiteboard with diagrams that he hoped to present to the community at the next meeting. In Jake's mind this was the way forward, and as someone who had always worked with his hands, both in a garage and towing vehicles, it felt natural to offer his help. Anything that would rebuild the community was worthwhile. And with Landon having returned, it would give him something to keep his mind off Sara.

After dropping off his bags at Sam's they made their way up to the second checkpoint at the intersection of Shore and Castine Road and informed the ten-man crew that was stationed there of where they were heading. Sam had built up quite a rapport with the militia, more specifically Ray. They admired what Sam had accomplished in Castine prior to Harris and his goons showing up. It was one of the reasons why they'd stuck around. That and because the community were willing to help. With Belfast being six times the population of Castine and the people opposing what FEMA was trying to do, they no longer had to worry about their safety as the city had already taken actions to protect their own. In Ray's mind that was all he wanted. Though Jake knew his interests in Castine ran deeper, they were linked to Teresa. Why he would want to jump into bed with her was a mystery.

"You think life will ever go back to the way it was?" Jake asked.

"You're asking me? You're the one with all the answers about this event."

Jake smiled and patted the horse's mane as they galloped. It would take at least four hours to reach the destination but they figured they'd get there before dark. When Jake didn't reply, Sam continued. "I don't think it will ever go back to normal. If government manages to find its feet, those in power will be held responsible and I don't think anyone will admit fault so... no. I think we will see a new country, one that is formed by the people. Who knows, maybe it will look something like the way it did when Columbus found America." He chuckled then his smile faded as quickly as it appeared.

It had been a long while since he'd ventured out of Castine. In seven months Mother Nature had taken back land that had once been covered by cement. Tall grass, weeds and wildflowers grew up through cracks in cement. In some areas, parts of the road had been swallowed by thick undergrowth.

They discussed many things on the way out to Ellsworth that day. He learned a lot about Sam, and likewise. There was so much that people kept to themselves. That was the one good thing about the blackout. The fall of technology and power had forced them back into real connections, talking face to face, having conversations that didn't involve texting or phoning. For those who were older it was a welcome relief, and for the young a shock.

"It's just up ahead."

They guided the horses down a dirt road with wooden fences on either side. Beyond that were fields upon fields of crops. As they came around a bend in the road that led up to the house, Jake's eyes widened. It wasn't the state of the home that caught his attention but what was hanging from a tree nearby.

"Carl!" Sam snapped the reins and the horse bolted up the remainder of the driveway. Jake already had his M4 Carbine out and was scanning the terrain for threats. Sam leapt off the horse and hurried over. Carl had been strung up by his wrists and stripped. At a glance it looked as if he was dead because his body had been cut all over. There wasn't an inch of his flesh that hadn't seen the sharp edge of a knife. It was a bloody mess. "Carl. Carl!" Sam turned. "Jake. Help me get him down," he said getting under his body and trying to support his weight. Jake brought the horse over and cut the rope and Carl slumped into Sam's arms. He patted his face a few times and Jake tossed down a canister of water to him. He splashed liquid over his skin then brought it to his lips.

"Carl!"

His eyelids snapped open and then he gasped!

Chapter 5

Bennington dumped the bullet riddled body of Lee Ferguson in front of Harris. His eyes widened in shock at the sight of him. It wasn't the death of a key member of the militia, or having him dragged in front of him that bothered him but the timing. He was supposed to receive a visit from one of the heads of FEMA that evening. For the past few months he'd been in contact with Brooke Stephens over in Waterville, Maine, which was a part of Kennebec County.

When the power grid went down seven months ago, FEMA was quick to respond with the usual six-phase protocol of disaster management which was supposed to cover prevention, mitigation, preparedness, response, recovery and reconstruction. They were meant to coordinate response efforts in conjunction with federal, state and local agencies.

They were damn good at it too except the country had

never experienced disaster at this level.

"What the hell is this?" Harris asked coming around his desk. "Are you out of your goddamn mind?"

He waved his hand toward Lee. "Proof. I said I would bring it. You can't get much better than this. You know who this is?"

"I don't care. Get him out of here. I have a very important meeting and the last thing I need is a dead body."

Bennington gave a nod to a few of his men and they dragged Lee out.

"A meeting? Tell me more."

"You are not invited."

Bennington took out a cigarette from his top pocket and lit it, and proceeded to blow smoke in Harris' face. "That was Lee Ferguson. The brother of Ray Ferguson, the head of Maine Militia." He stood there all smug like as if expecting a pat on the back or some form of applause.

Harris got close. "Let me make something very clear,

Bennington. The only reason you are involved is because of what you see on that board over there," he said pointing to the towns that were no longer under control. "How you fix it is up to you. But don't be bringing bodies back here. You will start a riot. There are already rumors circulating in this camp about what the militia have done. Folks are talking about leaving."

"So? Let them leave. It's one less headache," Bennington replied.

"You have no idea, do you?"

"Man. All I give a shit about is whether or not I have your support for what I have planned. So, do I?"

Harris stared at him with a blank expression. "You are reckless."

"But I get the job done."

"Get out. Don't come back until you have something better than a dead person to show me."

Bennington snorted and turned to walk out. "Oh, by the way. There is a cache of weapons that I managed to collect from the same place we went today. Seems law enforcement is alive and well. Well, they were until I dealt with it but…"

"Get out!" he said, glancing at his watch again.

Bennington smiled. "You still haven't answered. Do I have the support of the military for my endeavor this evening?"

"I told you to speak with the colonel."

"I already have. He's waiting on you."

"Then you have my permission. Just leave. Now!"

"All right. All right. But, oh, I forgot to mention something." Bennington turned around and looked at him. "When Castine is back under my control, I will work with you but the agreement will be on my terms."

Harris screwed up his face. "Your terms?"

"Hey. If you have a better way of getting these folks to dance then by all means, but from what I can see you have already tried and failed. So I figure that it's only fair."

"For who?"

"Both of us. You get to tell your friends in higher

places that everything is going according to plan, and not suffer humiliation, and I get to run Castine on my terms with your support."

"You think this is about negotiating?"

"Very much," Bennington said taking another hit on his cigarette.

He was such a cocky asshole but he had Harris by the balls. If they lost any more towns he would be relieved of his duties and while that would mean less responsibility, it would also mean fewer perks. And where he was positioned, he had access to anything he needed. He couldn't go back to being a civilian. He looked out at the mass of people in the camp. While their needs were met, what they received was limited, whereas he and his men had the best food, the best accommodation, the best of a world that was quickly sliding into ruin.

"What kind of deal?" Harris asked.

"You want 50/50. I will give you 30 and I keep 70, and I want some of your soldiers available to me."

Harris laughed.

When he could see that Bennington was serious, he said, "I don't make those calls. The military is responsible for their own."

"Really? And yet the colonel reports to you."

"How about you go and do what you say you can do, then we discuss it," Harris said, flicking his hand as if he was swatting away an annoying fly. Bennington didn't move.

"Or I could do nothing and you would have to explain to whoever you're about to have a meeting with why…"

"Okay. But we will discuss better terms once it's done."

"70/30 or I don't do shit."

Harris clenched his jaw. If he could release all the soldiers from the camp to head into Castine he would, but his hands were tied and he had his own restrictions. "60/40 and no more."

"That's a deal."

As Bennington left he saw a Humvee entering through the gates. It was her. Harris went back in and over to a mirror hanging from a tent pole. He adjusted his tie, and smoothed out his suit. He splashed on some cologne and ran his hands over his freshly shaven face. It was more than a meeting. So much more. Brooke Stephens had been on his radar for many years. A dark brunette with long hair, two years younger than him. He was hoping to impress her with his work in the three counties of Penobscot, Waldo and Hancock in the grand hope of getting a little closer... much closer.

"David."

He turned to find her in the entranceway of the tent. She was wearing dark slacks, tight black ankle boots, and a suit jacket with a white blouse. "Brooke. It's good to see you," he said hurrying over with his arms wide expecting to get a hug, instead she put a hand up and walked straight by him.

"Let's get down to it, shall we. What kind of progress are you making?"

Harris pursed his lips. He could see she was in no mood for relaxing.

"What's the hurry? Can I get you a drink?" he asked crossing the tent and holding up a bottle of gin, and a bottle of bourbon. She ignored him and moved toward the board where he had the towns listed and color coded.

"I hope you have good news."

"I do," he said sidling up beside her. "All of them are in check and on board, barring a few minor casualties."

"Is that so?" she said raising an eyebrow and casting him a sideways glance.

"Indeed it is. I mean, the casualties were unavoidable but we expected that, right? I mean with martial law being rolled out."

"They're all on board?"

"All of them."

"Then why have I heard that Belfast and Castine are not contributing to the efforts?"

His stomach sank. The thought of her dismissing him would be humiliating. He wouldn't be able to live that down. Harris pulled at his collar feeling his temperature rise. "A minor setback. Nothing we can't handle. In fact I have a group that is dealing with the matter as we speak."

"Dealing?" She turned to him. He nodded. "David, you are aware of how important this is and what is at stake here?"

"Of course."

"And I don't just mean your job. We are the arm of the government until the power grid works again. America isn't just relying on us for their basic needs, they are expecting us to lead with confidence regardless of how the circumstances around us change. Now when you received orders to enforce martial law, I didn't expect to return here and have to listen to you talking about *setbacks*. If you can't do the job, David, there are many who are more than willing and capable of stepping into your shoes. Do you understand?"

He gave a nod.

"Consider this a warning. I don't like having to come down heavy, especially since you are a colleague of mine, but mark my words. If it comes down to me or you, there will be no hesitation on my part." She lifted her nose in a snooty manner as if her shit didn't stink. "I think I will have that drink now." And just like that she was back to acting as though everything between them was fine.

* * *

"He just needs some time," Beth said to Dakota. "Anyway, how are you holding up?" she asked as they searched the cupboards for a pan they could use to cook the fish in. Dakota had gone through a range of emotions since her time on the AT. She hadn't discussed what had happened to her beyond the little she'd told Landon. The finer details she left out for good reason. It was her mental state that concerned Beth. Everyone dealt with trauma in different ways and she had gone to hell and back. Losing a husband and child, and being assaulted and held hostage on the AT was hellish. Beth could only imagine what that could do to someone's psyche.

"I'm fine," Dakota said as she rummaged inside a cupboard on her hands and knees.

"You sure?"

She poked out her head. "Beth. I appreciate you asking

but I'm handling it the best I can. What about you?"

"Me?"

"You lost someone too."

"Seven months ago."

"That's still fresh."

"Ah, I found one," Beth said holding up a pan. She set it on the counter.

Dakota looked out the window for Landon who was collecting wood from the surrounding forest for the firepit. "It's going to be strange living in a town again after all that time."

"Yeah," Beth said. "But it could be worse."

"Worse?"

She didn't have to say anything for Dakota to realize what she meant. The encounter with Billy was still there at the forefront of their minds. The dangers of a lawless country would always be there, an ever-present threat regardless of where they were. Town or not. Crazies looked for opportunities to take advantage of others and here would be no different. "I'm curious to find out what kind of infrastructure they have in place or if they'll listen to Landon's ideas."

"Pawling, New York, offers a good example of what's possible," Dakota said. "But I think Pawling had a lot more going for it by the sound of their preparation prior to the collapse. I think that factors into whether a town can rise from the ashes and rebuild."

"Rebuilding isn't the challenge," Beth said while getting some cutlery out. "It's preventing people tearing others down. Pawling had supplies. Food. The luxury of time on their side to ingrain good habits in the people. Most towns are going to have a hard time trying to convince others to get on board with rebuilding, especially if what Rita said about FEMA is true."

Dakota grabbed a few plates and laid them on the table. They were still getting used to the fact that they didn't have to worry about getting rained out. She welcomed the new pace of life, however different it would be.

Right then they heard a key in the front door and it

opened wide. Beth pulled her handgun and stepped into the hallway to see Sara standing in the doorway.

"You can put that away," Sara said in soft voice.

"Sorry. It's a habit."

She closed the door behind her. "Landon here?"

"He's getting firewood."

She nodded and looked around as if she hadn't been in her mother's home in a long while or was wondering if they'd touched anything. "We haven't been introduced. I'm Beth."

"I know. He told me."

"Right."

Sara stepped into the living room and Beth followed her in. Sara sank into a chair and put her hands together.

Beth thumbed over her shoulder. "I can get Landon."

"It's actually you I came to speak to."

"Oh." Beth clasped her hands behind her back. "Right." She turned to Dakota and told her she'd be a few minutes but to continue without her. There was silence as if Sara was contemplating.

"He said you brought Ellie's body back to your cabin. Is that right?"

She swallowed hard. "I did."

"She's buried there?"

Beth knew she'd already had this conversation with Landon so she assumed Sara was wanting confirmation or checking that he was telling the truth. "She is. Beside my father. Who died around the same time."

"I'm sorry to hear that." She looked Beth up and down. "How old are you?"

"Eighteen now."

Sara nodded. "Thank you for what you did. I never got to say that before you left and I just want you to know that it means a lot. Having him back and..." She looked into her palm.

"He cares a lot about you," Beth said. Sara lifted her eyes. "I don't know how much Landon has told you about our time on the AT but if it wasn't for him I don't think I would be alive. He's a good man."

"I know he is. It's just..." Sara trailed off.

"Complicated. I get it."

"How was he on the trail?"

A smile formed on Beth's face. "What version did he give you?"

"He didn't."

Beth took a seat across from her. She was a good-looking woman. She could see why Landon had fallen for her. It would be a pity to see them split over the circumstances of what they'd been through but then again maybe it would have happened regardless of the blackout. "Like I said. If he wasn't there. I'm not sure I would have made it."

"He says the same about you." Sara allowed herself to smile even though Beth could see she was troubled. "He hated camping. Always used to complain about it. We only did it once and that was enough. That's why it surprises me that he made it back in one piece."

"He nearly didn't," Beth replied. "I think there are a lot of things that would surprise you about him now." She rose. "You should speak with him."

Sara glanced at her watch. "I... I have to go."

"Sara. I'm not one to interfere but I hope you can work it out."

She lowered her chin a little. "I hope so too."

As she got up and headed for the door, Landon came in the back. "Sara?"

They looked at each other and Beth felt awkward as if she should have been elsewhere. He came in, wiping his hands on a cloth. "Are you staying for dinner?"

"I can't. I have to go. I just came by to drop off a few items that you might find useful," she said, removing a backpack and giving it to Landon. She opened the door and outside was Tess waiting on horseback. Before heading out she turned and looked at him. "Jake is gone. In fact a few people have gone from the house. You're welcome to return. I'm sure Max would appreciate it." With that said she smiled at Beth. "Nice to meet you, Beth."

And with that she closed the door, leaving Landon standing there staring into the bag.

Chapter 6

The atmosphere in the house that evening was somber. It seemed that Jake and Sam's departure had been the catalyst for others to consider returning home. Up until that day all fourteen rooms had been filled with different families that had opted to move into the Manor in order to work together versus going it alone. For a time it had worked. Each of them carried the load from fishing to cooking and cleaning to protecting the home. The Manor had started to feel like an island; a secure abode for those seeking shelter from the trouble that had besieged Castine. Now that was all changing.

"Jenna and Richard want to leave?" Sara asked Rita.

She nodded as she stirred a pot of rice outside in preparation for serving the meal. They had taken to cooking outside over a fire. Smoke rose up around Rita as she told her of a few other couples who were considering leaving.

"But they only arrived two weeks ago." Sara looked down at the flames licking up around the large pot and sighed.

"As nice as this is, it's not home, Sara. It's your home and people know that. They want their own space. And with Ray's guys patrolling and zero attacks in the last month they figure it's safe to return. And Jake and Sam leaving… well… it was to be expected."

"But we are stronger together. And we might not have seen FEMA trying anything lately but Bennington is still out there, and other groups. The whole point of inviting them in was to help them as much as it was to help us."

Rita shrugged. "I don't know what to tell you, dear."

"Well do you want to leave?"

"No. I enjoy the company but you should know that Janice and Arlo have been considering it. Now of course that depends on the meeting tomorrow night. Talk of alternative forms of power — wind and hydro — is giving people hope."

"Hope of light. What about hope of staying alive?"

She shrugged again and stirred the pot. "Here, give me a hand carrying this into the house," she said taking a cloth and wrapping it around one of the handles. Sara did the same on the other side and they lugged it into the kitchen where Tess was scraping salad into bowls.

"You leaving too?" Sara asked.

She looked up. "Where would I go?"

"You have a house."

Tess frowned. "What's the matter?"

"Rita will tell you," she said. She set the pot down and walked out. Although she didn't want people to leave, she couldn't exactly stop them.

"Max. You up there? Time for supper."

"I'm skipping it tonight. Already eaten," he said. "I'm actually going out."

"Where?" she hollered up. Nothing burned her more than trying to have a conversation with him via the staircase. She liked to look into someone's face as there was a lot that a person could hide and lately her trust in her son or better put, her trust in what Ray was filling his head with, was at an all-time low.

"Heading over to Ray's."

"That's the fourth night in a row. I'd like you to join us for dinner."

"Dad returned?"

"No," Sara replied.

"Well I'll head out and go see him."

She couldn't exactly argue with that. The fact that he wanted to see or speak to him after learning about Ellie was a miracle. "All right. Just don't come home late. Be back by eleven."

"What if I decide to stay the night?"

She groaned. He had a point. "Well are you?"

"Don't know."

"Look, Max, can you come to the top of the stairs? I hate talking to a wall."

She heard him trudge along the landing and then he appeared at the top of the stairs.

"We're not going through this again, are we?" she asked.

"What?"

"You know full well what."

He sighed. "I'm going to see dad, okay? I might be back tonight; I might be back in the morning." There was a pause. "I'm eighteen, Mom."

She threw up a hand. "You know what — do as you please. Everyone else seems to be." With that, Sara shook her head as she walked back into the kitchen to help.

* * *

Max returned to his bedroom where Eddie was waiting. "We good to go?"

"Golden," Max replied, scooping up his bag and climbing out the window. He'd got in the habit of exiting that way to avoid confrontations with his mother. Although he hadn't spoken with his father yet since he'd returned, he was beginning to wonder if she'd driven him away.

"So we're heading to your father's?" Eddie said when they landed on the ground and took off toward the shed to collect the bikes.

"No."

"But you told your mother."

"What she doesn't know won't hurt her. We're going to do some recon on the FEMA camp."

Eddie shook his head and stopped walking. "You said we were going to speak to Ray about getting some gear, then you said visit your father. Now you want to travel to the FEMA camp? Look, man, I'm all for doing dumb shit but even I know when to draw the line. What's the purpose?"

"Gather intel. Do what these guys aren't. Gain some respect. Right now everyone including my mother thinks I'm incapable of making smart choices but the fact is if it wasn't for you and me, that dick Bennington would still be in charge. Now of course we could have died and maybe it was a bit reckless but no one can deny the outcome."

Eddie threw up a hand. "Ah, I don't know, Max. That's a long trip and how do you expect to get by the checkpoints?"

"By boat. We'll go around and up the Penobscot River this evening. I'm not waiting for permission. The fact is Ray still treats me like a kid. Hell, everyone does and yet we are the ones that have changed life on Castine. Anyway, tonight we'll get a few rifles from Ray's place and then head out."

"And if they try to stop us?"

"They won't."

Ray and his guys were using the ship called *The State of Maine* as their main outpost down at the harbor. It didn't take them long to reach it. Derek Nolan was one of the militia in charge of watching over the dock and keeping out those who didn't have permission to board. He and five other guys saw them coming but because of his involvement with Ray, they waved them on in thinking that they were there to see Ray. As they boarded the vessel, Max looked over his shoulder.

"They never said a thing," Eddie muttered.

"I told you."

As soon as they were on the boat he made a beeline for

the armory and collected two rifles, some NV goggles and some flashbangs. Crouching, Max tucked ammo into his bag while listening to Eddie discuss his theory on why FEMA hadn't attacked when suddenly a soldier appeared in the doorway.

"What are you two doing in here?"

Max turned and quickly answered. "I got the all-clear by Ray. We're helping out with a recon group heading up to FEMA."

"Recon? Why wasn't I told about this?"

"Speak to Ray. It was a last-minute decision. Anyway," he said looking at his wristwatch, "time's ticking. Gotta go." He went to walk past him when the soldier placed his hand on his chest.

"Wait." He got on the radio. "Nolan. You hear anything about a recon up at the FEMA camp?"

"No. Why?"

A smirk formed on the soldier's face as he looked back. "Max here says Ray okayed him to collect some gear from the armory."

"I don't know about that. Stand by. Don't let them go anywhere."

Max scowled. "Oh come on, man. You are gonna look like a complete fool when he radios over to Ray and confirms it."

"And Ray will tear me a new one if he doesn't. You just hang tight," he said taking a few steps back and blocking the doorway. Max looked at Eddie. He knew the moment they spoke with Ray they would shut them down and he couldn't afford to have that happen. All the pussyfooting around and treading lightly was starting to wear his patience thin.

"Look. We're just gonna go. I don't have time for this," Max said trying to go around him only to have him grab his jacket.

"Take a seat!" he growled shoving him back into Eddie.

"You know I'll have you demoted for this," Eddie said. The guy chuckled. Right then over the radio, Nolan replied.

"There is no recon group. Hold them there, we're coming up."

Max knew they had only seconds. If they didn't take action, the militia would strip them of gear and toss them off the boat. He glanced at Eddie and made a gesture. Eddie shook his head as if trying to persuade him not to do it. As the guy reattached his radio, Max lunged at him knocking him back. "Eddie. Grab his gun!"

Eddie reacted, cursing as he did it. "Damn it! We are so dead."

It all happened within a matter of seconds. One minute the guy was armed, the next he was staring down a barrel. "Now we're just gonna walk out of here and you can get in there," he said pointing to the armory.

"You won't get off this boat."

"You wanna bet?" Max asked.

Max removed his radio and then shoved him into the room and locked the door. Moving quickly they took a different exit, avoiding the group that was coming in from the stern. As soon as they were topside, Max looked over and saw a few of the guys still blocking the ship's gangway. He hurried along the main deck all the way to the end and then looked back.

"Can you swim?"

"Max."

Without explaining, Max tossed the bags and rifles they had to the shore. They landed on top of a stack of crates covered by a large tarp. Then he leapt over the side of the boat, dropping into the water. That was the wrong thing to do. The water was freezing. As soon as he came up, he gasped and looked up. Eddie was still on the boat. "Come on," he said beckoning him to jump.

"You are going to be the death of me."

Eddie climbed over the barrier and dropped, letting out a yell on the way down. As soon as he broke the surface and came up they swam to the shore and clambered up onto dry land. Soaking wet, and moving at a crouch, Max made his way over to the bags and rifles and they got the hell out of there before the others raised the alarm.

"You know how much trouble we are gonna be in."

"If I could have got this gear another way I would have."

"Ray will go ballistic. You have probably just ruined whatever relationship we had with them. Just when we were making progress. Now I'm going to be demoted."

"Demoted? You don't even hold a rank. They're not the military, Eddie," he said as they collected their bikes. They pedaled away from the docks as fast as they could.

"No but they're the closest to it." He groaned. "Now we're soaking wet and..."

"Stop complaining. Man. You bitch a lot. Sometimes to get shit done you have to think outside the box."

"Oh you thought outside the box!" Eddie bellowed.

"Look, we'll head back to my place, get some dry clothes and head out."

"Uh do I have to remind you of what happened the last time?"

"Eddie. Give it a rest. This is Ray not Bennington."

They continued pedaling fast, taking a few shortcuts

back to the Manor. However, by the time they made it back, Ray and several of his men were already at the Manor. "Okay, what now, smartass?" Eddie asked hiding in the shadows.

"Screw it. We'll dry off in a few hours," Max said turning to leave.

"Are you serious?"

Their clothes were already sticking to their skin and Max's boots were still filled with water. "Yes. Unless you want to try sneaking past them?"

They stood beside their bikes in the tree line watching Ray and his men enter the home. "Let's wait it out. He won't hang around long and then we can sneak in, get fresh clothes and head out."

"All right," Max replied. He was more than willing to just continue on but he knew he wouldn't hear the last of it. Eddie would chew his ear off complaining.

"Tell me something," Max asked while they waited. "How come you haven't gone home in over a week?"

Eddie shrugged. "My parents don't care where I go."

"Really?"

He stared at him. Eddie was terrible at lying.

"They're dead, aren't they?"

Eddie glanced at him. "Look, I think we should get going."

"Don't dodge the question. Eddie. What happened to your parents?"

"It doesn't matter. We need to…"

"Eddie!"

"All right. Yes. They're dead."

"That's why you were at Nautilus."

He gave a nod.

"Why didn't you tell me?"

He shrugged. "I don't know. Didn't think it mattered. You had enough on your mind with your father and sister gone."

"How did they die? And when?"

He went quiet and ran a hand over his face. "Three weeks into the blackout our home was raided. At least that's what I think happened. I was out at the time. Over at Nautilus Island. When I returned I found them shot and everything was taken from the house. I didn't have much choice but to head back and stay on the island." For the first time since Max met Eddie, he didn't have a smirk on his face.

"Man, you should have told me."

"And how would that have helped?"

Max stared back at him dumbfounded. "You wouldn't have had to carry the burden alone. That's a lot of shit to handle. And then that whole thing with your brother."

"I don't want anyone's pity," Eddie said hardening his face.

"It's not about pity," Max said. "This. Me and you. The only way that works is by being honest."

"Yeah, like you were really honest about your father and sister."

"That's different."

"Is it? You dodge the questions when I try to ask you about them."

Max gritted his teeth.

"Not easy, is it," Eddie said. "Much easier to avoid than speak about it."

Max gave a nod then looked toward the house. Ray and his guys got on their horses and took off. "All right. Let's make this quick," he said. "After this, we get the boat and head up the bay."

"What are you hoping to achieve from this, Max? Even if you find out something new, Ray isn't going to listen."

"Maybe not but the community will."

Chapter 7

The engine went quiet and the fishing boat glided effortlessly through the water under the cover of darkness. Bennington and three men observed the shore of Castine coming into view. "Okay, listen up. You know the plan. In and out. Martinez, you clear?"

A soldier with a buzz cut and hard features nodded.

Rob Martinez was clothed in Lee Ferguson's fatigues.

As the bow of the boat banged gently up against the rocks, Bennington hopped out and held the front while the others climbed out. Waves lapped up and a fine mist blew in off the water. Mick dragged the boat ashore with the help of Jenkins and Ryland and they covered it with branches before heading inland. They trudged through the forest on the west side of Castine heading for a farm located just off Mill Lane. It was home to Benjamin Willis and his wife. Mick specifically picked their property as he knew Willis wasn't the kind of man to stay quiet and this relied on someone who wouldn't back down. Mick figured that they'd only have to do this two or three times to get the community to look at the militia in a different light. No one knew Rob, he had never visited Castine, but they were familiar with militia uniform. It was a different shade of camo to the ones used by the military working with FEMA.

The only reason Mick was there was to make sure it all went off without a hitch. As they got close to the home, Mick heard a dog that was tied up outside bark. That could be a problem. They crouched in the darkness.

From the tree line, he removed his NV binoculars and scanned the windows of the home. The inside of the home was lit up by candles. Flames flickered, casting shadows on the wall and revealing the occupants. A woman in her early forties passed by with a cup in hand and took a seat beside Ben.

"So you approach the main door. Tell them you are performing a routine check and draw the guy out. Ryland and Jenkins will handle him then you go and do what I said."

"I'm not killing her."

"I didn't say you needed to. But we need to send a clear message."

Rob frowned but headed toward the house. Ryland and Jenkins got into position while Bennington shrouded by shadows watched from the tree line. Rob gave a knock on the door and waited. He looked over his shoulder then the door opened. A quick exchange and Ben shouted into the house something and then stepped out. Rob led him around the house. Bennington didn't see his two guys strike but he knew it was done when Rob reappeared without Ben. He gave the thumbs-up and headed into the house. From there, Bennington heard yelling, items being smashed, a woman scream, and five minutes later Rob came out with two rifles slung over his shoulder. He hurried toward the tree line where they were waiting for him.

"It's done."

"Good man," Bennington said as they returned to the

boat. Next they would swing around to the south end of the island and commit the same, two more times that evening. No words were exchanged on what had been done except that he hadn't assaulted her. That was the only thing Bennington wouldn't have them involved in. It wasn't required and was an evil that not even he could bring himself to commit. Instead, Rob entered, confiscated weapons, took a few supplies and trashed the place. Ben had been knocked out and left behind the house for his wife to find. Bennington had given Rob instructions to tell her that Ray Ferguson had ordered that all weapons be removed and that from now on he would be rationing out supplies. It was just the kind of act that would incite the community, cause people to point the finger and throw doubt on the assistance of militia. A few additional incidents like this and FEMA wouldn't have to drive out militia, the community of Castine would do it for them.

* * *

Dry, energized with some food and ready to set off for

the FEMA camp, Max and Eddie had not only eluded Ray's men and his mother but they'd managed to make their way down to Dyce Head to collect the boat without anyone seeing them. "I have to admit, Maxy boy, I thought the gig was up back at the boat but you once again surprised me. However, we are pushing it this time."

"Don't worry, they'll thank us for it."

He stopped walking and looked at the spot where they'd stashed the boat. No. No! It was gone. Max hurried over and lifted some of the large branches. Beneath it was the camo netting. "What the hell?"

"You two are just too predictable."

Max spun around. "You really must take me for a fool," Ray said stepping out of the tree line with several of his guys. "And I thought you were better than this, Max."

Both of them backed up but there was nowhere to go except in the water or back up the steps that snaked up the side of the cliff — and those were blocked off by one of his guys.

"I just wanted a few pieces of gear."

"Why didn't you ask?"

"Because I knew you'd say no," Max replied.

Ray shifted from one foot to the next and stared at him. "Let me guess. You were planning on doing some recon on the FEMA camp or were you going to turn yourself in?"

Max didn't reply. A couple of Ray's guys lightened their load by taking their backpacks and the rifles they'd taken from the armory. Ray got closer to him. "I just don't get you." He paused for a second. "Actually, let me rephrase that. Yes I do. You're a kid who doesn't think," he said tapping Max on the side of the temple.

"You wouldn't even be here if it wasn't for me."

"Really? Clyde. Did you hear that?"

One of his guys smirked.

"Max, you've obviously forgotten. You came to us for help. So no. The only reason YOU are here is because of us. Right now Sam, Jake, your mother. All of you would have been under the thumb of FEMA and the military had it not been for us. So how about you show me a little fucking respect!" He grabbed a hold of Max by the shoulder. "You ever pull any shit like this again, and you'll find yourself at the bottom of the bay. Do I make myself clear?"

Max didn't reply fast enough so Ray bellowed in his face. "Do I?"

He nodded.

"Get the fuck out of here."

"What about my boat?"

"Your boat has been confiscated. There are consequences."

"And the guns?"

"We'll hold on to those for now."

"That handgun belongs to my father."

"Yeah, well, now it belongs to me," Ray said. "If he wants it, he knows where I am." Ray turned to leave but Max wasn't done. He lunged at Ray and in an instant removed his handgun and pulled back holding it out in front of him. It even caught Eddie off guard who backed away telling him to put it down.

"Do as he says, Max."

"No. I came this far and you are not getting in the way."

"In the way of what? Huh? What? What are you hoping to achieve?"

"What you guys haven't achieved."

Ray shook his head and smiled. He wasn't intimidated by Max in the slightest. "Tell me, Max. Do you get to eat three times a day? Do you sleep without worry of being attacked?" He waited for an answer. "You have us to thank for that." He extended his hand. "Now give me the damn gun."

Max shook his head.

"Max, just give it to him," Eddie said. Even he was taking Ray's side.

"No."

Ray ran a hand over his face. "Kid, killing those two people who invaded your house must have really done a number on your brain. We are on your side. Now give me the gun."

"Fuck you. I'm tired of being told what to do."

"Is that what this is about? Little Max trying to prove he's a man. Is it?" Ray took a few steps toward him and his hand began to shake as he placed his finger on the trigger.

"Back up, Ray! I'm warning you."

"Okay. You want to be a real man? Pull the trigger. Go on! Take us all out."

"Back up!" Max said as Ray took a few more steps toward him shaking his head.

"You want to shoot me Max? Huh?" He stepped forward again. Bay water splashed against the rocks beneath their feet making every step even more precarious than the last. He'd heard of people slipping and being washed out by the strong undercurrent. "Go on, Max. Squeeze the trigger!" He stepped forward again until the barrel of the gun was pressed against Ray's chest. When he knew Max wasn't going to do anything he disarmed him in an instant. "That's right. You don't have the balls to do it. And there was me thinking you were militia material. You are nothing but a scared little kid."

"I'm not a kid."

"No? Then stop fucking acting like one." He turned to Eddie. "That goes for you too."

He offered back a dumb expression, raising a hand. "Hey, I was just—"

"Doing whatever he said. That's admirable but stupid under these circumstances."

Ray inserted the handgun back into its holster. He lifted his hand as if he was about to swat Max around the face. "I should beat you black and blue. Knock some sense into your pinhead, but I get a feeling that wouldn't help." Ray shook his head in disappointment before turning and heading back up the steps leaving them alone. "And Max," he shouted over his shoulder. "If I have to come and chase you down again, I won't be as lenient next time and I don't give a fuck what your parents will say."

Max sighed and kicked some loose stones out of the

earth.

"Well that's that," Eddie said. "You want to go back to your place and smoke a doobie?"

"Is that all you can think of?"

"At least we won't get our asses handed to us."

Max brushed past him.

"Where you going?"

"Home."

"Sounds good. I'm coming."

"No. You know what, just… just give me some space."

Max left him there with his jaw hanging. He knew he didn't have family and would probably return to Nautilus Island but right now he was in no mood for his wisecracks or company. He wasn't just pissed off that he'd failed but pissed off that Ray was right. He still hadn't grown up. He was still making reckless decisions and in turn being treated as someone who couldn't be trusted. He knew he should act better but he no longer cared. Ellie wasn't coming home. His father… well… they'd never been close. He just thought he could make a difference, prove himself to Ray, to a group that he admired and be accepted as one of them but he'd just done the reverse. *Stupid. So stupid.* He gave himself a slap on the side of the face.

When he made it to the top of the cliff, he trudged back up Battle Avenue with a heavy heart wondering what Ray had told his mother when he'd swung by earlier that evening. The last thing he needed was to have her on his back. He figured he'd slip in through his bedroom window and go up to the attic and sleep in the secret room. At least there he wouldn't get hassled by her and it would give him time to think up an excuse.

* * *

In less than fifteen minutes he was home. Climbing the trellis, he grumbled under his breath. His thoughts turned to his father and the discussion they would no doubt have. Once he was on the roof he noticed there was a light emanating from his bedroom. A flicker from a candle. *Great.* His mother had seen him and now he was about to get the third degree from her. "You know I really don't need this tonight," he said as he climbed through his bedroom window to find Beth perched on the edge of his bed reading one of his magazines. They looked at each other and she smiled.

"Always enter your house through a window?"

He hopped down onto the floor and frowned before taking the magazine from her hands. "Maybe. What are you doing in my bedroom? I thought you were staying at my grandmother's?"

"I am. I thought I would swing by and chat."

His eyebrow raised and a sudden wave of embarrassment came over him. If she'd found this magazine, what else had she come across? He tucked it back into a drawer, placing it on top of the Playboy mags, and turned to find her looking amused.

"Does my mother know you're here?"

"She does. I figured you'd be a no-show but… here you are."

"Here I am," he said slowly placing his hands behind his back and looking around the room for anything else that might cause him further embarrassment. He spotted a pair of dirty underwear and quickly scooped them up and stuffed them in the closet. His cheeks went a bright red. Since her arrival they really hadn't spoken except for small talk. The weather. Good morning. Good night. The usual awkward exchange when he didn't know someone.

"So... what did you want to chat about?"

Chapter 8

Jake exited Carl's room early that morning with the doc. They'd returned from Ellsworth in the early hours of the morning and informed Ray's guys to let him know that his brother had been murdered. "So, how is he?" Jake asked.

"He's in pretty bad shape, that's for sure." Doc Summers, thirty-nine, dark hair and tall, had been a physician operating out of Bucksport but his home was in Castine. "He'll need frequent monitoring so I will stick around for today and tomorrow, if that's okay?" he said turning to Sara who was nearby. She nodded. "For now I've given him something for the pain, and set up an IV. I've done what I can but without a hospital his condition could get worse."

"Okay, thanks, doc," Jake said patting him on the shoulder.

"There's coffee and breakfast in the sunroom," Sara

said. "Help yourself."

He thanked her and headed down the hallway, leaving the two of them standing outside the first-floor room. Jake yawned and rubbed his eyes. "You should get some sleep," Sara said.

"Yeah. How are you holding up?" he asked.

"I'm fine."

He cocked his head and she pulled a face. "Okay. I'm not exactly having a good day but compared to what Carl just went through I think my troubles are minor."

"Finding out you lost your daughter isn't minor, Sara," he said.

She nodded but didn't look as if she wanted to get into it. They ambled toward the sunroom to get some coffee. It was just after seven and the few remaining people in the home were just beginning to stir. "Did I tell you that we are down to Tess, and Rita now in the house?"

"What? The others left?"

"Yesterday," she replied stepping into the sunroom. Doc had filled his cup and taken a seat on one of the sofas. "I guess your leaving was the catalyst."

"Ah Sara, I'm sorry. I just felt it was the right thing to do with Landon back and all."

"You're not at fault. It was going to happen one way or another. People think it's safe. Obviously not. I tried to tell them but you know how folks in this town can be. Besides, I get it. I don't think I would want to be anywhere else."

"Now you bring it up, I was thinking. With all that happened. The location of Castine. Have you considered moving out of town?"

"And go where?"

"I actually have a cabin up near Caribou Lake, north of Bangor."

"Yours?"

"It used to belong to my parents. I only went there a couple of times a year. But I was thinking it might be safer than here."

Sara pulled a face as she filled up her cup with hot coffee. "Thanks, Jake, but I grew up here and I plan on dying here. Besides we are close to the water and people I know. I couldn't leave them behind."

"They could come too."

She shook her head and was about to reply when Max walked in all chipper. "Morning, Jake. Morning, Mom. Morning, doc." He had a spring in his step that looked strangely out of place when compared to his usual shuffling. He'd also removed his beanie, and was wearing a shirt she'd bought for him a year ago but he'd never worn.

She narrowed her eyes. "What's got into you?" she asked.

"What? Can't someone feel cheerful?"

"Yeah. But you're usually dragging your feet and looking like the whole world is against you."

Max poured himself coffee and brought it to his nose and sniffed. "It's a new day." He smiled and Jake's gaze bounced between them.

"Has this anything to do with Beth who dropped by last night?"

"Beth?" Jake asked.

"Yeah, the girl with Landon. She stopped by last night and wanted to speak with Max."

"Is that so?" Jake asked getting a big grin on his face and bringing his own cup up to his lips to take a sip. Now it all made sense. It was astonishing the effect a girl could have on a guy. "I thought I recognized that expression," he said.

"What expression?"

Jake patted him on the back and was about to take a seat when a door slammed. "Where is he?" Ray's voice carried. They heard Rita reply and then boots pounding the hallway.

"I should go and make sure things are okay."

Sara nodded and he set his drink down and set off. He hadn't spoken to Ray since they'd left for Ellsworth. He could only imagine why he wanted to speak with Carl but Carl was in no state. Drugged up on heavy meds he was already asleep when Ray charged into the room demanding answers. Jake managed to get there just as he was trying to shake Carl awake.

"What happened to my brother? Huh?"

Jake rushed in to help Carl. "Hey. Hey. Ray. Leave him alone."

He had to forcefully pry Ray's hands loose from Carl's collar. Carl's eyelids were heavy and he was barely able to summon a reply, let alone one that would have been logical. His memory of the incident was foggy at best. Carl sank back into his pillow as Jake dragged Ray out and slammed the door behind him. "What the hell are you playing at?"

Sweating profusely as if he'd run to the Manor, Ray came straight back at him. "Four of them went and only he came back? Doesn't that strike you as a little odd?"

"Did you see the state of him?"

"I want to know what happened."

"And you will but for now he needs to rest."

Ray clenched his jaw and balled a fist as if he was about to strike Jake.

"Look, the little I managed to get out of Carl was that

Bennington was behind this. Him and a group of reserve soldiers showed up and ambushed them. They didn't stand a chance."

Ray turned to leave. "Then I'm going to get his body."

"Don't bother. They took it."

He spun around. "What?"

"Carl saw them take Lee with them."

His brow furrowed. "So he's alive?"

"No. He's dead."

Ray looked confused, shell-shocked. "Then why would they take him?"

Jake shook his head. "No idea. I just know that we need to increase the security in Castine."

Ray lifted a finger. "No. We need to strike back." He turned and headed down the hallway cursing. Jake took off after him.

"Hold up, Ray. You're not thinking clearly."

"I've never been clearer."

"If you go charging at that camp they will open fire and more lives will be lost. Do you want that?"

He stopped walking and jabbed a finger at Jake. "I want those bastards to pay." Tears welled up in his eyes. It was the first time Jake had seen him show any emotion beyond anger. The militia had survived this long because of smart decisions and good leadership.

Jake placed a hand on his shoulder. "And they will. Okay? They will. But we need to talk with the others, plan, strategize how to do this, if at all."

"If at all?" He studied Jake's face in a way as if he couldn't comprehend him. "That sounds to me like you've already given up."

"Is staying alive giving up?"

He gritted his teeth. "Let me tell you something. I didn't come this far to back down now. Lee would turn in his grave if he knew I did nothing. I won't stand by and do nothing."

Jake closed the gap between them to make it clear that he wasn't afraid of Ray, nor was he intimidated by the bellowing in his face. "I'm not saying do nothing. I'm saying that these kinds of things are all about timing."

"Jake, you ever served?"

"No."

"And yet you want to tell me what to do?"

Jake took a deep breath and blew out his cheeks. He ran a hand over his head. "I might not have served but I know nothing good comes from reacting in the heat of the moment. Just take some time."

"Did Bennington take time killing my brother?"

That shut Jake down in an instant. Ray backed out of the house but then returned a moment later. Jake was still standing where he left him. "How did he know?"

"What?"

"How did Bennington know?"

Jake shrugged. "I don't know."

"Exactly. The only people who knew about that run were Carl, Sam and..." He trailed off, a look of shock spreading across his face. "That bitch." With that said he hurried out. Wherever he was going, it wasn't good. Jake took off after him but by the time he got outside, Ray was already on his horse and leaving with four of his men.

Jake knew better than to intervene any further.

As they were leaving, Eddie came pedaling like a madman up the driveway.

"Hey Jake! You seen Max?"

He jerked his head toward the house. "He's in the sunroom."

Eddie barreled past him not slowing for even a second.

* * *

Max was sipping on coffee relishing thoughts of his conversation with Beth from the previous night while his mother chatted with the doc. Outside the sun was rising high in the sky spreading a warm orange glow through the clouds. It was gonna be another beautiful day. Except this one seemed even better than the others. Lost in thought he smiled causing his mother to frown again. He hadn't felt this good in God knows when. It wasn't that the conversation with her was anything significant but something about being around her made him forget the world had gone to shit. It shouldn't have affected him but he couldn't help but feel upbeat and positive that morning.

Out the corner of his eye he spotted Eddie swerve around the house and drop his bike, yelling something. "Oh great, what now," he muttered.

"Max. Isn't that your friend?" his mother asked.

"Yeah, yeah," he said getting up to cut him off before he entered the sunroom. Knowing him he'd open his mouth and get him in trouble, and after slipping under the wire with his mother over the visit from Ray the previous night, he was looking to avoid any unwanted trouble. He figured his mother would have grilled him after last night but Ray hadn't mentioned the theft of property or that he'd pursued them, instead he only said good things, which only added to the feeling of guilt that Max was carrying.

Still that was then. This was now.

"You gotta see this."

"See what?"

"Just get your bike. Let's go."

"I haven't had breakfast yet. I was just enjoying a nice

cup of coffee," Max replied, smiling. Eddie caught it. He hadn't known him a long time but he knew him well enough to know that smiling was generally at the bottom of the totem pole in his world.

Eddie frowned. "What's the matter with you?"

Max shrugged. "Nothing's the matter."

"No." Eddie nodded. "Something's off with you. You changed your hairstyle?"

"No."

"Changed your clothes?"

Max chuckled. "I do shower."

"Could have fooled me." Then Eddie stabbed a finger at him. "That's it! You changed your clothes. You're usually wearing black but…" He stepped back. "Is there a full moon tonight?"

Max decided to nip this conversation in the bud before it circled around to Beth and he had to go into fine detail about his interaction with her which Eddie wouldn't believe amounted to conversation only. He'd want to put some weird sexual spin on it.

"Eddie. Shut up. What do you want me to see?"

"The cache of weapons. The ones that went missing. I know where they are."

"Finally remembered, did you?"

"No. I know who took it."

"Well then why didn't you say when we were over there?"

He waved him off heading for his bike. "Not then. Last night, after I left you, I decided to head back to the island."

"But my boat was gone and Ray left yours out in the water."

"I found one."

"Found?"

"Borrowed," Eddie shot back before grinning.

Max rolled his eyes. "Okay, so... you found it. Whoopee doo. What does that mean to me?"

"I didn't get it back. I... well, I was hoping you would help with that."

"Man, I was lucky my mother didn't ream me out this

morning."

"Oh yeah, how did that go last night?"

"Well I didn't speak to her because Beth…" Her name shot out of his mouth before he realized.

Eddie caught it. His eyes narrowed. "Beth? Go on. What were you about to say?" A sly grin formed.

"I meant my mother."

"No, you said Beth. There's a big difference between mother and Beth. C'mon, you old dog," he said lifting his bike up and staring at him waiting for an answer. When he didn't give it, Eddie continued. "She came over, didn't she?"

Max couldn't help but smile. He must have looked like a Cheshire cat.

"Oh please tell me you did the double backed beast."

"Double back….? Eddie. Shut up, man! Is that all you think about?"

"Please. A girl with an ass like that shows up in your house and you—"

"My bedroom."

"What? Hold on. Your bedroom? Oh that's even better. And you're telling me you did nothing?" He raised his hands all theatrical, like he was conducting an orchestra.

Max ran a hand over his face as they strolled over to the bike shed to collect his bike. "You think we can get back to the part where you tell me who took the cache of weapons?"

"Oh right. Yeah. Probably best I just show you. You packing?"

Max grabbed his own crotch. "Always!" then started laughing.

Eddie thumped him on the arm. "Idiot."

They collected his bike and headed for the harbor. Eddie had stolen some small fishing boat from a home not far from the lighthouse. It was slightly smaller than the one he had before it was confiscated by Ray but at least it would get them across the choppy waters.

There was an air of excitement to Eddie's conversation that morning as if he'd consumed one too many cups of coffee or hit the jackpot. Max didn't fully understand why until they made it to Holbrook Island Sanctuary. The nature preserve on Penobscot Bay near the town of Brookville was often used for hiking and cross-country skiing. A huge area of land covered in forest, meadows, and wetland marshes was the last place Max expected to find those responsible for the theft.

Chapter 9

Rage blocked out common sense as Ray dismounted outside Emerson Hall. He charged through the main doors with all the urgency of a police officer but he wasn't there to protect. As he approached Teresa's office, his men stepped out of the way, knowing better than to try and stop him. He burst into the room to find Teresa sitting in front of the ham radio. She glanced at him and muttered something then signed off. "Ray."

He slammed the door behind him and locked it.

"Who was that?" he asked gesturing to the radio.

Teresa's brow knit together. "A colleague."

"Yeah? As in Bennington?!"

"No."

She backed up behind her desk as if sensing the threat.

Ray swung a hand across the desk sliding off paperwork, a mug of coffee and her scheduling book. It clattered on the hard floor and liquid splashed against the filing cabinet. "Don't lie to me!" he bellowed.

"I'm not."

He jabbed a finger at her. "I've known for some time you've been conversing with Harris. You even admitted it. But Bennington?" He paused for a second to catch his breath. "What did he promise you for telling him about the ammo run?"

"I don't know what you're talking about."

"Don't lie!"

She lunged toward her drawer and he let her slide it open. It was empty. "Looking for this?" he said removing a firearm from the small of his back. "I took it a while ago. Had a feeling you might try to use it one day." He stuck it back into his waistband and made his way around. She backed into a corner.

"I'm warning you. I can have you removed."

"Removed?" He laughed. "You have zero authority in this town anymore. No one trusts you. No one likes you. Everyone thinks you're a bitch."

"Yeah, well this bitch pulled the wool over your eyes."

He lunged forward and grabbed her by the throat. "I just lost my brother because of you."

"GET OFF ME!" she yelled as he squeezed harder.

Suddenly from outside the door there was knocking. "Ray. It's Sam. Open up."

"Sam!" Teresa yelled.

Ray continued. "You think anyone will give a shit if you're dead?" He threw her down on the floor and began choking her while Sam beat on the door. Seconds later, the door burst open, parts of the frame spat across the room like a blast from a shotgun. Sam soared over the desk and yanked Ray back. "Leave it. She's not worth it."

"It's because of her Lee's dead."

"Ray. She'll be dealt with but not this way."

Ray shoved back, launching Sam across the room into the wall. In that split second of distraction, Teresa got up and was clambering over her desk trying to escape when Ray latched on to her ankle and dragged her back to the floor. "Ray!"

"She's been communicating with Bennington via the

ham radio."

Sam lunged at Ray and wrapped an arm around his neck and put him in a chokehold just to get him off her. Teresa was coughing and spluttering, her face red. Had he waited any longer she would have passed out. Ray thrashed in Sam's grasp. A couple of Ray's guys appeared at the door and looked as if they didn't know what to do. "We can use her. Listen to me. We can use Teresa!" Sam shouted.

Then as if a light came on in his head, Ray stopped struggling. His body went limp.

"Are we good?" Sam asked. Ray nodded. He released his grip and Ray rubbed his throat. As Sam rose, Ray lashed out and cracked him on the jaw sending him back against the wall. "You ever do that again. I will kill you. You understand?" Ray said.

Sam wiped his lip with the back of his hand. "Listen to me for two damn minutes. We can use this to our advantage. She's no good to us dead. You want payback, you'll get it but killing her isn't going to bring back your brother… but keeping her alive might give you Bennington. I want him as badly as you do." He wiped his face again and took a seat. "Fuck, you got one hell of a punch," he said opening his mouth and rubbing his jaw. Ray waved off his men and took a seat across from him, every few seconds he would give Teresa dagger eyes.

Sam turned to Teresa. "What's Bennington up to?"

"I don't know what you're talking about."

"Don't bullshit us, Teresa. You've been playing both sides since they arrived."

"Why would I do that?"

"Because you're a bitch," Ray said. "I swear I should just put a bullet in your head."

Sam put a hand out. "Relax." He looked back at Teresa. "You want to see tomorrow then you'll do exactly as we say. You understand?"

She pursed her lips and scowled at him.

Sam shook his head. "Really? You want him to shoot you?"

Teresa looked at Ray who was one step away from the

edge. "What do you want?" she asked.

"Harris. You're gonna bring him here along with Bennington."

She snorted and continued rubbing her neck which was bright red. Sam could see the outline of Ray's fingers on her skin. "He won't show up, not with Ray here."

"Then you'll tell him he's gone. That after finding out that his brother was dead, he pulled all his men out. You'll tell Harris that you want Bennington back in his position and that I've gone with Ray. All of us have."

"He won't believe it," Ray said.

"Maybe not but it should create enough curiosity for him to send a few guys this way. I imagine Bennington will be one of them. That's who shot your brother. That's all I care about. Harris. He's just a scared puppet."

"I won't do it," Teresa said.

"Then I guess we have no reason to keep you around." Ray pulled his firearm and Sam was quick to get between them.

"Wait."

"C'mon, Sam. She's playing us like fools. You really think she's going to feed them to us? I say we get rid of her and attack the camp."

"Yeah, that sounds smart," Sam said sarcastically as he got up and went over to the ham radio, took the mic and extended it out to Teresa. "Well?"

"I told you, I'm not doing it. You can kill me if you want but I'm not playing both sides."

"You already have," Ray said.

"And you haven't? Sleeping in my bed. What was that about. Love?" she said in a taunting fashion.

Ray shook his head. "Fuck it. I'm done with this cow!"

Sam grabbed his wrist but couldn't prevent him squeezing the trigger. The gun went off shattering the window behind Teresa's head. "Enough! We can do this. Just listen." Once he saw Ray had snapped out of it, he turned to Teresa.

"Get on that ham radio now and tell Bennington that we are having a meeting tonight to discuss leaving. We'll plant the seed. He'll at least buy that after what's happened. From there we'll figure it out tonight."

Realizing that Ray wasn't messing around, Teresa turned and reluctantly picked up the mic.

* * *

Max assumed Eddie was taking him on another wild goose chase. He had visions of arriving at some clearing in the sanctuary to once again find him dumbfounded as to where the cache had gone. Except that wasn't the case this time.

Hiking through the old woods and across rocks lined with thick, verdant moss and carpeted with orange pine needles, Max got a sense that someone was watching them. "Are we getting any closer?"

"Yeah, it's just over this rise."

"You said that four times."

"Geesh. Someone's impatient," Eddie replied.

As they came over a rocky stretch, Max could smell a fire, and hear voices. Eddie motioned for him to get low to the ground as they came up to the top of the steep incline and took cover behind a large collection of boulders. "Down there," he said. Max scrambled up to get a better look. That's when he saw a fire pit and a group of around twenty. It was hard to tell how old they all were from their position as some of them were hooded, others looked as if they were teenagers though. One of the campers pulled a rope and Max's gaze shifted up into the tall pine trees. His eyes widened at the sight of wooden catwalks that snaked between the trees and tiny huts.

"Who are they?"

"Well they're not Ewoks, that's for sure," Eddie said cracking a grin. "But those bastards have my weapons."

"Yours?" Max asked.

"Ours. You know what I mean."

Max squinted. "Why are they here?"

"Do I look like I know the answers? I don't care why they're here. Maybe it's an orgy. I just want to get my hands on our gear."

Max grumbled. "Well I don't see it."

Eddie pointed. "Over there, do you see that container?" It was a Rubbermaid box with a white X painted on the side. "That's mine."

"And you know this because?"

"The X on the side. X marks the spot."

Max shook his head in disbelief. "X marks the spot? What the hell are you talking about?'

"You know, like hidden treasure. X marks the spot. I marked the container."

"Oh my God," Max said in a slow voice before sighing. "Your stupidity knows no end."

"What?"

"You're meant to do that on a map, or on a tree nearby, not on the actual thing you're burying. Uh!" He looked back at the ragtag group who resembled a tribe.

"Well sorry for getting it wrong. Geesh. Anyway, the point is that's ours."

Max crawled away.

"Where you going?" Eddie asked.

"You're not getting those back. We should leave."

"Leave? But we just got here?"

He shrugged. "I have things to do."

"Like what? See Beth?"

Max turned and his brow furrowed. "No. But I have better things to do than scour the woods and risk my ass trying to get back some empty box."

"We don't know it's empty."

"Oh please. Come on, Eddie. You're wasting my time. I'm not going down there and risking my life."

"Oh but you'd risk mine and your life heading up to the FEMA camp. And you say I'm stupid. Well you're not too bright yourself, buddy." He turned back toward the camp. "You know what? Even though your idea was stupid, I said I would go with you. So thanks. Thanks for nothing." Max stood there looking at his back. He groaned then trudged back.

"All right. How do you want to do this?"

Eddie raised a brow. "The old-fashioned way. We head in there and call them out on their shit."

"You are joking, right?" Max replied.

He shrugged. "No."

Max raised a finger and cleared his throat. "You want

us to walk into a group that we don't know anything about and just ask for the weapons back."

"I'm not asking for permission. I'm telling them we're taking them back."

Max patted him on the back and chuckled. "Well best of luck with that plan, my friend."

Once again he turned to leave.

"I thought you were gonna help?"

"I thought you had a better plan."

"I do," Eddie shot back.

"No you don't."

"Do you?"

Max stopped walking. "Yeah, we leave."

"I'm not leaving until I have those guns."

Max grit his teeth. "Well then at least sneak in under the cover of darkness."

Eddie got up from the ground and made his way down the slope, pitching sideways as he came. "Look, if you think sneaking in at night is better than my idea, you are a dumbass. That's a surefire way to get shot. Whereas if we go in there and speak to them, man to man, I'm sure we can reach some agreement."

Max stared back at him. He couldn't believe he was about to agree to his asinine plan. He gave a muted sigh. "Okay."

"Okay? You'll do it my way?"

"Yep," Max said in a nonchalant manner, raising a hand. "Lead the way."

"Hold on a second. You're going to do it my way?"

"Yes. And hurry up before I change my mind."

Eddie grinned, puffed out his chest as if he had won some world champion chess match. They turned and headed down into the unknown.

They didn't make it far.

Fifty feet from the camp, bodies dropped out of trees all around them, a few areas of the forest floor flipped up and the sound of guns being cocked could be heard all around them. Both of them raised their hands. "Damn it Max, I told you this was not the way to the massage parlor," Eddie said out loud. None of them cracked a smile.

Within seconds, they were grabbed and thrust forward toward the camp. All eyes were on them as they were shoved through a crowd. "Do you mind?" Eddie muttered.

"Caine!" one of them bellowed.

A lean guy with a buzz cut emerged from a tent. He was wearing a black V-neck T-shirt, tight jeans, combat boots and had a handgun strapped to his thigh. His muscular arms were all tattooed up with Chinese letters that reached his neck. Slung over his shoulder was an AR-15. Following behind him was a female with long dark hair who was dressed in a tight black leather jacket, and yoga pants with boots similar to Caine's. Eddie leaned into Max and whispered, "I bet you any money that gun is ours."

"Quiet," Max whispered.

"What have we got here?" Caine asked, a smile dancing on his lips.

"They were approaching from the west."

Knowing Eddie was liable to put his foot in his mouth, Max was quick to answer. "We're from Castine. Sorry to barge in but my friend here says it appears you have something that belongs to us."

Max looked around the camp and could now tell how old they all were. They couldn't have been over twenty-one. There were no adults, so to speak, at least from what he could see.

Caine took a step back and grinned. "Is that right?"

"Damn right it is," Eddie said pointing to the box. "I buried that and hid it well."

"Obviously not well enough."

"Anyway, hand it over and we'll be on our way."

Caine stared back at him with a blank expression. He looked at a girl beside him and then burst out laughing. "Get a load of this guy. Hand it over and we'll be on our way," he repeated Eddie's line before snorting. The others around joined in laughing. "Man, you two have got some serious kahooners to come waltzing in here." He walked over, took a large knife from a sheath on his hip and pointed it at Eddie. "And what if I say no. Huh?"

"Well, all is fair in love and war. I had to ask. No problem. You keep them. I was thinking of upgrading anyway." Eddie turned to leave and was pushed back.

"Upgrading." Caine burst out laughing. Eddie joined in. Then as quick as a flash the smile vanished from his face and Caine burst forward bringing the knife up to Eddie's throat. "You think this is a fucking game?"

Max tried to intervene but was quickly struck in the ribs with the butt of a rifle by another camper. His legs buckled and he coughed hard. He gazed up at Eddie who looked as a white as a ghost. "Leave him alone," Max said.

Caine grabbed the back of Eddie's collar and thrust him toward a group of his guys. "You two just made a serious mistake."

Chapter 10

The town hall meeting was set for seven-thirty that evening. Landon had got word of it on his way over to the Manor that morning. They'd crossed paths with a flustered looking Sam who was on horseback with four others telling those in the community. It would have been a lie to say he wasn't interested in seeing what kind of setup they had in town. From the little he'd gleaned so far it looked organized but appearances could be deceiving.

"I'll be there," Landon replied.

Sam took off and they stood there in the middle of the road wondering what the hurry was. It didn't take long to shift his focus back to his own troubles.

Although Landon was a little hesitant to go back to the manor, he figured if he and Sara couldn't resolve their differences, he could always return to her mother's home. Though he hoped they could. He'd come to realize over the course of his marriage that holding grudges, and drawing out conflict for long periods of time never did anyone any good. His mother who'd been religious would often quote some pithy passage from the Bible about not letting the sun go down while you were still angry. Growing up in a family where religion was the center of everything they did, it took him until his late teens to appreciate the wisdom of that line.

"So what did Max say?" Landon asked Beth as they walked on Shore Road. A light breeze blew in off the ocean, bringing with it a few memories of better days.

"He said he would swing by today. That was before you decided to head back. I'm sure he'll be pleased."

"Huh," he said shaking his head.

"What?" Beth asked.

"You continue to surprise me, Beth."

"I'm sure there was more to it than that," Dakota added with a smile.

Beth gave her a playful slap on the arm but said nothing.

"Am I missing something?" he asked.

"Oh nothing important," Dakota said. "Isn't that right, Beth?"

Beth simply smiled.

"You two are confusing me." Landon scooped up a stick from the underbrush and tossed it for Grizzly. He bounded away and returned with it in his mouth. Beth took it the next time and ran ahead with Grizzly, getting him to jump by holding the stick at hip level.

Dakota turned to Landon. "You sure about this?"

"About?"

"Returning so soon after leaving. I don't think I could do it."

"I've been married a long time, Dakota. I have to give Sara the benefit of the doubt. Besides, under the circumstances it's very possible that could have been me."

She shook her head. "Not me. When I get involved, I'm all in 100 percent. I can handle the bad days but if Mike had ever cheated on me that would have been it. No excuse for that."

"Seems a little black and white, don't you think?" He

reached for a long piece of grass and stuck it between his lips. As a kid he'd enjoyed chewing on blades of grass. Something about the texture. Probably wasn't good for him but then neither were cigarettes.

"The way I see it. You get into a relationship to be with that person. If you don't want it anymore, leave them and move on. Only cowards try to play both sides of the fence."

"Look, I'm not coming to Sara's defense here but… I think the human heart can be a little more complicated than that."

Her brow furrowed. "How so?"

Landon looked at her. "You date many people before Mike?"

"No, I knew him since school."

"That explains a lot then."

"Like?" He thought she seemed offended by his remark.

"I mean you have nothing to compare it to and so you see it the way you do. Had Mike cheated on you and you got involved with someone else or had you suddenly felt strong feelings for a co-worker while married, you might grasp it."

"Grasp it? You did not just say that."

He smirked. "What?"

"Grasp it? As if I need to grasp something. Like you're trying to school me."

He chuckled. "C'mon, you know what I mean."

She smiled but he could tell she genuinely was pissed at what he said. "No. No I don't."

Landon groaned. "Do I need to explain?"

"I think you should," she shot back.

He took a deep breath. "Um. How do I put this? The heart wants what the heart wants."

"That's one way of putting it Landon but it sounds to me like a way to justify cheating, or a means of escape from a life of boredom with a partner you committed to."

He chuckled. "There really is no gray area with you, is there?"

She shrugged. "I just see things the way they are. If

someone wants in, get in. If you want out, get out. But don't play games. It's tiring and life is too short," she said. "Besides, when you say the heart wants what it wants, you sound like you are speaking from experience." She paused. "Are you?"

"Am I what?"

"Speaking from experience. Have you had desires for others while married to Sara?"

He could tell he had just opened Pandora's box and there was no way of closing it now. "I think we should catch up with Beth."

She stabbed a finger. "I knew it." She chuckled.

"Knew what?"

"You have. You've had feelings for others while married. That's the only reason why you are not bouncing off the walls, and the only reason why we are heading back to the Manor." Landon stopped walking. Dakota continued for a few more steps before turning. "Well, am I right?"

He lifted his gaze to the baby blue sky and narrowed

his eyes. "You're too smart for your own good," he said grinning.

She laughed. "C'mon then, who was it?"

"Look, I didn't kiss her. I knew where to draw the line but…"

"But…?" Dakota asked fishing for details.

"I got emotionally involved. There. You happy?"

She nodded, grinning. "Details. More. I want to know."

Landon continued, "For someone who shuns it you sure seem to be eager to hear about it." He waved her off. "Maybe later."

"There might not be a later. Why not confess your sins now?" she said jokingly.

He roared with laughter. "Dakota, you are something else. But I think I've already said enough."

"Oh come on, you can't leave me hanging now. So you didn't kiss this woman. Who was she? Where did you meet? How did it end?" She peppered him with one question after another. He groaned.

"I was away from home a lot, okay! Sara and I were going through one of our rough patches. The woman, Emily, worked at the same place as me."

"The ferry business."

"Yep. I met her a few times and… I don't know… something seemed to connect between us. She was funny. Attractive. She didn't want anything from me. And I guess I felt under the thumb at home. Anyway, Emily had just got out of a bad relationship with another guy and maybe we were able to relate on some strange level." Dakota listened intently as if his tale was like some daytime soap opera. "It started out as very innocent. Just two co-workers enjoying chatting. I found myself falling for her. I couldn't get her out of my head. I wanted to talk with her every day. Just seeing her smile made my day. Then like any fool who gets lost following his heart, I started to think that perhaps me and Sara weren't cut out for one another. That there was a future with Emily and I."

"So it became an obsession?"

"Obsession is too strong a word. Fascination. Lust. Desire, Whatever makes us go a little crazy. And believe me, the only time I have acted like a fool is when I've been in love."

"So you loved Emily?"

Landon pulled a face. "Love? What is that anyway? A feeling? An action? It seems everyone and his uncle has their ideas about what love is. All I know is that I had strong feelings for her. I wanted to be with her. I just thought if we could meet that I would be able to tell. You know. Like if she was right."

"Hold on a second. You never met her?"

"No. I met her multiple times just not at that time when this happened. Our communication was through the phone, messaging and whatnot."

Dakota grimaced. Landon didn't blame her. As he looked back on it now, it was kind of stupid to lose his head over a woman but the truth was she didn't seem like any old woman. Emily was something else. The conversation flowed effortlessly.

"Hence the emotional tie," Dakota said. "Got it."

Landon continued as they strolled past the bay and several locals on horses rode past them. One of them he recognized as Pat Stephens, an old friend of his. Pat waved and he gave a nod.

"Anyway, I figured if I had such strong feelings for someone other than my wife that I should do what was best and end it with Sara."

"But you didn't."

He shook his head. "No. No I didn't."

"Then how did it end? I mean with Emily?"

"Emily was younger than me."

"Aren't they always," she said rolling her eyes.

"Hey, she wasn't that much younger. We're not talking half my age. A few years max."

"That's a first," she replied. He wondered why he was telling her all of this and what good could come from it. But he noticed that it was helping him. It had weighed heavily on his mind for years. Even though he hadn't kissed or slept with Emily he couldn't help but feel a sense of guilt, that he'd kept this a secret from Sara.

"So…?" Dakota asked.

"She did what any woman who was single would do. She used her common sense and started dating someone else. And made it very clear that I was not in her future. In some ways she did me a favor. Who knows what level of stupidity I would have dropped down into had I followed through with what my heart was telling me."

"Was it your heart or that thing between your legs?" she muttered, a grin forming.

"Hey. I'm a hot-blooded man like anyone else. But it wasn't about that. I mean maybe it would have been, had it gone further, but I genuinely enjoyed her company."

"The woman you never spent time with."

"I know. I know. It sounds stupid. But when you talk to someone as frequently as we did because of my work, well, you might find yourself falling for them especially if you connect over your mutual relationship issues." Landon shrugged. It made sense to him.

"But you were married."

"Ugh. Forget it. Some things people either understand or they don't."

She stopped walking this time and he kept going. It was only when he noticed she wasn't coming that he cast a glance over his shoulder. "What?"

"Just because I haven't had that experience it doesn't mean I can't understand it."

"Well you seem like you've already judged me."

"Oh and you haven't judged your wife?"

Landon shook his head. "This is why I didn't want to get into it. You're getting all high and mighty about it now. The next thing I know you'll be throwing scripture at me."

"I don't have a religion."

"That's good to know but it hasn't stopped you from throwing shade my way," he said. Their conversation had now made its way to Beth's ears. She had stopped walking and was looking at them having a spat. Dakota hurried to catch up with him. He could tell this wasn't going to end well. "Look, Dakota, can we just drop it? I really don't need this right now."

"Yeah. Sure, but don't treat me like some naïve little girl without any experience. Believe me I've dealt with my fair share of troubles."

"Really? Like what? And don't say losing your husband and child as I think…"

The words shot out of his mouth so fast and he immediately knew it was wrong but she was pushing his buttons — making him feel guilty for what millions had done all over the world. Of course, those who had an idealistic view of relationships wouldn't agree but he hadn't shared it with the hope that she would teach him the proper way to be in a relationship. He already knew. Relationships could be beautiful and ugly all at the same time. A mixture of lofty expectations and tragic letdowns.

"You want to go there?" she asked.

"Might as well, as I haven't heard a peep out of you about what you're going through and yet you are all so eager to know how I was coping with losing Ellie, or what I think about Sara's mistake."

"Maybe it wasn't a mistake. Have you thought about that? Maybe she wants to be with Jake. Are you prepared to walk away if that's the case?"

He chuckled. It was hard to believe they were arguing about something that had nothing to do with her. They must have sounded like an old married couple to Beth who had now made her way over to intervene. "Guys. Guys. Can you hear yourselves?"

"I can hear myself very well. Dakota, I'm not so sure. She sure loves the sound of her own voice."

"Oh nice. Who's judging who now?"

Landon shook his head and picked up the pace to put some distance between him and her. Thankfully Dakota didn't push the issue any further. They continued on the rest of the journey in silence, arriving at the Manor a little later than he had hoped for but that was to be expected with all the bickering.

As they came up the driveway, Landon stopped walking. Standing outside tending to a horse was Jake. "You've got to be kidding me," he muttered under his breath. He considered turning around and heading back but Jake saw him so he continued on.

Jake must have felt the awkwardness of the situation as he was quick to point out that he wasn't staying and had just dropped by to update the home on the meeting for the evening. Landon just smiled politely and walked into the house. He heard Beth outside talking with Jake as he made his way down to the kitchen.

"Landon," Rita said. "You're back."

"Yeah. Not sure for how long," he muttered looking over at Sara who was nursing a cup of coffee. In all truth he couldn't blame her because to do so he would have to tell her of his own mistake. Then again was it a mistake? Perhaps Dakota was right. His relationship with Sara hadn't exactly been a bed of roses, more thorns than anything else. They had good times but he wasn't sure there was enough there to hold them, especially after seven months apart.

Chapter 11

Escape was impossible. They were tied to posts in the center of the camp, always under scrutiny from the campers. If it wasn't for the fact that they weren't dead, he might have been worried but as it stood they had been kept alive for a reason — he just hadn't figured out why.

"This is so humiliating," Eddie said, going red in the face.

Max cast a glance sideways to see his pant leg soaked. Eddie had told them he needed to go for a piss but they just thought it was a ploy to escape.

"Ah, could be worse," Max replied.

"How could it be any worse?"

"You could have shit yourself," Max replied without a smile.

"Really? Really, Max. I don't think this is the time to be cracking jokes. This is serious. We might die out here and no one will ever know."

"You should have thought of that before you charged ahead."

"Oh this is on me?"

"You wouldn't listen," he said observing some blonde who had been eying him since he'd arrived. She was sitting by a fire using a knife to sharpen a stick. There was something very primitive to their way of life, yet he hadn't observed anyone eating wild game. In fact he saw them eating out of MREs.

"You mean to your great plan to sneak in here under the cover of darkness?"

"Could have worked."

"Could have, would have, you're not helping!"

"Just saying…"

"Don't say it."

"I told you so."

"I told you not to say it," Eddie replied.

He would have shrugged if his restraints weren't so tight. Both of them had their hands tied behind an eight-foot wooden post jammed into the ground. He had no idea what it was for as there were three of them but they were spread about four feet apart and close to the firepit where the campers could keep a close watch on them.

"I'm just saying walking in here wasn't a smart idea."

"Oh that's right, you're the king of being tactically sound. Go ahead, why don't you beat your chest and tell me some of your war stories, oh great leader," Eddie said. "Oh that's right! You don't have any."

"You don't need to have been in the war to know that they weren't going to listen," Max replied. The blond girl smiled at him and he returned the gesture hoping that it might give him leverage. He watched her lean in to a girl with braided red hair beside her and they both looked over and chuckled.

"And yet you agreed to go with me," Eddie said.

"Well, what kind of friend would I be if I just let you go alone?"

"What? Am I supposed to be grateful?"

Max smiled again at the girls, and Eddie must have noticed this time as he was quick to jump all over that.

"You've got to be joking. Are you flirting?"

"Maybe," Max said, a smile dancing on his lips.

"Well don't! Besides, there's no time for that. We need to figure out how to get out of here before that lunatic Caine returns and decides to peel the flesh from our bones."

"What do you think I'm doing?" Max replied giving his best *'let's hook up'* eyes.

Eddie's eyes bounced from Max's to the girl and back again. "Huh. Come to think of it, that might work." He smiled too and the two girls scowled at Eddie. Max burst out laughing.

"Seriously, you need to work on your game."

"Game? I've got game," Eddie spat back.

Caine emerged from a tent and made his way over. He had an apple in his hand and was chewing in a sloppy fashion. Eddie immediately went into some spiel about why can't we all just get along and let bygones be bygones. It was quite amusing.

"I've been doing some thinking about the cache. How

did you end up with it in your possession?"

Eddie shot Max a look. "Does it matter? They're yours. Enjoy. Now if you could just untie this—"

"Shut up!" he bellowed in Eddie's face, covering his face in spit and chunks of apple. "I wasn't talking to you." He looked back at Max and got a little closer. "For someone that is in a very precarious position, you don't look at all scared."

"Should I be?" Max asked.

"Very much so," Caine replied.

Max pulled a face. "I guess in seven months I've come across my fair share of dicks, what's one more?"

Caine sneered and removed his knife in an attempt to intimidate him but it wasn't working.

Despite his reluctance to go into the camp with Eddie, Max really didn't give two shits whether he died or not. It was the reason why he agreed. Sure, there was Beth now but from his experience, nothing good that was worth a lick of salt lasted in his world. And this whole event had only proven that.

"Where did you get the weapons?"

"From your mother," Max replied. Caine smiled then lashed out striking him in the face with a hard fist.

"You want to go down that road? Oh I can accommodate."

Max spat blood on the ground. "Does that accommodation come with a jacuzzi because I've always been fond of…" Before he could finish, Caine struck him again then lifted the knife to his neck.

"Go on. What were you going to say? I'm just aching to do it."

Blood trickled out the corner of Max's mouth. "And yet here I am. Still alive," he muttered, taunting him before spitting out a mouthful again. Caine snorted then pulled back his hand to strike him again when the girl with blond hair hurried over and whispered something into his ear. Caine took a step back and they had an exchange. Max tried to make out what they were saying but could only catch a few words. Certainly not enough to get the gist of it.

He shot Max another glare and pointed at him. "We'll continue this later."

"I do hope so. Maybe you can remember to bring someone who hits harder." He smirked, flashing red teeth. Caine stormed off, yelled to some of those in camp and they disappeared into the forest. The blonde stood there for a moment before turning to him.

"You know you really shouldn't taunt him."

"Why because underneath that rough exterior he's a big teddy bear?" Max replied with a grin.

"Actually he is. The name's Lindsay."

She smiled and shifted her weight from one foot to the next, her eyes looking him up and down like an ice cream.

"I also come in three other flavors," he said. "But we can talk about that when you loosen these restraints."

She pursed her lips. "Um, I can't do that."

"Come on. You can't honestly agree with this?"

"I don't but it's for our safety."

"We're unarmed."

She stared at him. "Roughly a month ago we had a group stroll into camp. A lot like you two. They just wanted a bed for the night, some food and they'd be on their way the next day. It nearly cost us the life of a friend of ours." She motioned to a bearded fellow across the way who was peeling potatoes. He had a black patch covering one eye.

"They killed one of ours, and carved out his eye while we were sleeping. Had it not been for the quick actions of Caine, they might have done a lot more damage."

"Sorry to hear that," he said in the most unenthusiastic manner. "And forgive me if I don't shed a tear but welcome to the blackout. Shit happens."

"That's right. And that's why you're tied up," she said turning to leave. "And if I were you I would be careful what you say to Caine. You're lucky you're still alive."

"Lindsay."

She looked over her shoulder.

"We just wanted the weapons."

"Everyone wants something," she replied.

"And you?" he asked. That got a confused look out of her.

Her brow furrowed. "I'm not sure I follow."

"What are you all doing out here?"

She turned back to him and reached into her pocket and removed a stick of gum. She unwrapped it and popped it into her mouth. "Everyone you see here has lost a parent, a brother, a sister or an entire family to disease, hunger, but mostly brutality. Caine brought us together. He created this place. Somewhere that's safe. Off the radar of towns and cities. Most people don't come here. You really have to go out of your way to find us. It's safe. People respect him for that."

She went to walk away and he said, "I lost a sister. Who did you lose?"

Without looking back she replied. "Everyone."

* * *

"So was it a success?" Colonel Lukeman asked Bennington.

"We shall see."

Lukeman got up from his chair shaking his head. "Why do I have a feeling this isn't going to work?"

"Oh, ye of little faith." Bennington had his feet up on the desk and was sipping on hot coffee.

He sighed. "Harris should have left this to me."

"Why would he, you didn't perform well in Belfast, did you?"

Lukeman narrowed his gaze. "Let's not forget if it wasn't for me and my guys you'd probably be lying in a pool of blood. Show me some respect."

Bennington laughed. "Anyway, where's Harris?"

"He got a radio transmission from Castine."

"He still banging her, is he?"

"That's none of your business."

"No. I guess not. So who's the legs?" he said gesturing with his head to the dark-haired woman. "Looks like she's taking over."

"Brooke Stephens. One of the higher-ups at FEMA. Her visit with Harris didn't go well. She wasn't impressed with the way things are being handled, hence the reason why Harris is banging, as you so bluntly put it, your town manager."

"She's not mine. Heck, if I had my way I would put a bullet in her head. From what I can tell she's playing both sides of the fence. I don't trust her."

"Well at least that's one thing we both agree on," Lukeman said. He removed a cigar from his mouth and blew out smoke as he stood by the entrance to the tent. "But you know how he is. I've tried multiple times to get him to rethink, approach this from a different angle but he won't listen. Meanwhile my men are dying because of it."

"I'm curious, Lukeman. Why are you still taking orders from him?"

Lukeman looked at him. "Because I was assigned here. It's my duty."

"No. It *was* your duty. Times are changing, soldier boy," Bennington said getting up and heading over to the A-frame. "Dwindling resources, soldiers going AWOL, the end is written on the wall my friend, no pun intended." He pointed to the map of the towns. "By this time next month, there will be two, maybe three more towns digging their heels in the ground. What then? I mean, Castine is just a blip on the map. Don't you want something more? Surely you have family?"

"I have my orders."

"And you're good at following them. I admire that. Though there is no fucking way I would have joined the military. Having people bark at me and tell me how high to jump. No. I'm just wired differently. Now, if it was me giving orders. Well, I might be open to that but..." He looked at Lukeman who was fixated on the camp outside.

Since his arrival, Bennington had been studying the hierarchy in the camp, observing the interactions between Harris and the military, because after losing friends at the hands of the militia he figured the only way forward from here was if he could rally a new group together, people that were used to taking orders, people that were capable and skilled and used to risking their ass for the great red, white and blue. He'd taken every chance to chip away at

Lukeman; understand him and find a common ground, but he was a difficult man. Still, he wasn't giving up.

"So. Family?" he probed again.

"Single," Lukeman replied.

Very good. No ties. Nothing to draw him away.

Bennington took a deep breath. "I admire your dedication though I have to wonder if it's a little misplaced."

"What do you mean?"

"Well," Bennington motioned to the map. "You've been at this... seven months, right? And what do you have to show for it? You sleep in a shitty tent; you work hours upon hours taking orders from a pinhead who wouldn't know his way around a gun if you stuck one in his face. What are you getting out of it? And don't say a sense of serving the country or any of that bullshit spouted by army guys when they return from tours. As you know as much as I do that no one cares, especially your government. You're just a number," he said pointing to his uniform. "Once you've put in your time, someone else comes along and replaces you and the wheels on the bus go round and round," he said making his way over. "Surely you want more than that? I mean, don't get me wrong, right now you think you have the respect of your men, hell, the respect of every person in this camp, but do you?"

Lukeman frowned. "I don't live for the applause."

Bennington laughed. "Please. Be honest, Lukeman. We all do. Just some of us are willing to admit it. The rest are just trying to impress others by acting like they don't. Reality is no one cares," he said patting him on the shoulder. "A month, maybe two at the most. All those people out there are going to know what a fuck-up this is and what will you do then? Try to control them? No. You know that would be futile. You see, the only thing we really can control is ourselves. So why not work for ourselves?"

"Are you suggesting I go AWOL?"

Oh he had him. He could see the look in Lukeman's eyes. A waning of interest in the camp, in following

Harris' orders, and being a puppet on a string for a government that had collapsed. This was progress. A chip here, a chip there, every interaction was shaping his outlook on the future. "AWOL would imply you walked away without official leave. When was the last time you spoke to anyone who was from the military?"

Lukeman smiled. "A long time ago."

"What kind of infrastructure do you know exists beyond this and other camps?"

"I don't."

"Exactly. And do you think that if the lights would come on tomorrow that anyone would care if you left your post?"

He narrowed his gaze at Bennington. "What are you suggesting?"

"I'm not suggesting anything. God forbid I give you orders. That's not my way. But I am asking you what you want? Has anyone asked you that? What do you want, Lukeman?"

Lukeman took a deep breath. "I want you to stop

filling my head with doubts. How about we start there?"

"Doubts? No. I'm a realist. The power grid won't be turning on. If there is one thing the people of Castine have right, it's that holding out hope for the government to come in and save the day is a joke. It's built on a faulty premise, and I can tell in my short time here that FEMA is one step away from losing its grip on these people. What happens when that happens? Who do you think they will turn on first?" He patted him on the back. "Chew it over, soldier boy." And like that he walked out of the tent with a smug grin on his face.

Chapter 12

The tension in Emerson Hall that evening could have been cut with a knife. Sam observed the knot of locals as they squeezed into the room. Many remained in the corridor because there just wasn't enough room. He sat at the front of the room with a small group that were in charge of taking notes, questions and complaints. Ray hadn't taken his eyes off Teresa for even a second since she placed the call to Harris. He scanned the faces noticing that Sara was distracted by Landon because he was eyeballing Jake. That was a disaster just waiting to happen. The only two that weren't in attendance were Eddie and Max. He could only imagine what they were doing.

"Okay. Let's call this meeting to order," Sam said rising to his feet. "If any of you have questions there will be time to answer those at the end of the meeting, in the meantime I'd appreciate your attention while we get through what we have to tonight." He looked down at his paperwork where he'd outlined some of the bullet points he needed to go over. "As you're all aware we have been working closely with Rodney Jennings to see the introduction of wind and hydro power. Rodney is confident that with the assistance of a group he can have something together within the month. Rodney, did you want to add anything to this?"

He shook his head and shriveled back into the crowd.

"Will it power every house?" a woman asked.

"Initially no. It will be used for the main center of operations at the Maritime Academy. There will also be a small hospital set up there. Depending on what Rodney has in mind, and how quickly we can get our hands on the material he'll need to build all of this, we should start to see homes powered again within the year."

"Within the year?" someone bellowed. "Are you kidding me?"

"Resources will be focused on the elderly first, and the young. The rest of us will have to wait."

"What a joke."

"Sir. The fact that anyone is doing anything is a miracle. Now if you don't like it, you know where the door is."

The guy got up and flipped the bird at Sam and stormed out.

Sam was unfazed by it. "That goes for anyone else. This community owes you nothing. Anything that is done to improve your lives is a bonus. Appreciation goes a long way but if you want to grumble and act like a self-entitled asshole, then the best of luck to you. We don't have time to deal with drama queens."

The guy who'd left returned and cursed at Sam before kicking a chair on his way out. People just got out of his way. There was no point in trying to stop him unless he tried to hurt someone. Sam had learned that lesson from the last meeting they'd had when he attacked Bennington.

"We are trying to rebuild a community. It's not easy especially with FEMA breathing down our necks and wanting to take what we have."

"Yeah, what is the deal with that?" Ally Stephens asked. "We haven't been required to hand over 50 percent in quite some time. Have they backed off?"

"I wouldn't say that," Sam said. He looked over at Ray and Teresa. "We recently came under attack."

"What?" A slew of people began talking among themselves. "Why didn't we hear about this?" "When did it happen?" The questions came hard and fast.

"Because it occurred outside of Castine. Three of our guys are dead," Sam said being honest with them. "We know who is responsible and we've taken steps to ensure it doesn't happen again but..."

"How?" someone shouted.

"How what?"

"How are you ensuring it doesn't happen again?"

He looked at Ray and he gave a nod.

"Ray and his crew will be leaving."

"What?!" There was uproar. He knew it would happen. The only thing keeping these people steady was the knowledge that the militia were protecting the town.

"It won't be permanent. It's a temporary solution until we can bring those who killed three of our own to justice."

"And by justice you mean killing them?" an older lady asked.

"We will do whatever is necessary."

"And does that involve stealing our weapons and destruction of property?" Benjamin Willis squeezed through the crowd followed by his wife. Both of them looked as if they had been through the wringer. With bruised and cut faces they garnered the attention of everyone. Behind them a few other locals muscled their way in with similar injuries.

Sam frowned. "What are you talking about?"

"I'm talking about Ray's guys hitting our homes in the dead of night. Stealing our weapons and roughing up my family. Our home is in ruins because of you."

Sam looked at Ray. "Care to shed some light?"

Ray rose from his seat. "I think you are mistaken. We

haven't touched you or your property."

"Really? You think we did this to ourselves?" Benjamin turned and two more families stepped forward and recounted what happened to them. "They were wearing the same uniforms as you!" he said jabbing an accusing finger.

Ray was quick to jump on those accusations. "Go on then. Which one of us did it?"

They turned and looked over the faces of his crew. Not all of them were there as there still needed to be folks manning the checkpoints. "Well they're not here but it was definitely you. They said you were taking supplies and weapons."

"I never ordered that."

Once again there was uproar. Sam shifted over to Ray and whispered in his ear. Ray nodded and looked back at Benjamin. "How many of my men were there?"

"Several."

"How many were wearing the uniform?"

"One."

He clenched his fist and cast a glance at Sam. "I had nothing to do with this but we think we know who is behind it."

"Bullshit. It was your crew." Benjamin tossed a water canister at Ray. All hell broke loose as Ray's guys rushed in and those in attendance, specifically the families who had just shown up, fought back. Somewhere in the hustle and bustle of it all, Sam noticed Teresa was no longer in the room. "Ray. Where is she?"

They turned and scanned faces. Ray bellowed for a few of his guys to check outside while he went for the closest exit near the back of the room. "Oh yeah, that's it. Run!" Benjamin said. "See, I told you."

They had it all backwards. Sam took out his gun and fired a round into the air drilling a hole in the ceiling. "Enough!" he cried. "You've got this all wrong. We've been set up. Bennington was behind this."

"Oh, that's a good excuse," Benjamin said pressing forward, pulling out a tire iron from inside his coat.

Sam raised his gun at him. "Put it down. Now!"

"You going to shoot all of us, Sam?"

"No. Only you. Put it down."

Benjamin stared at him before dropping it on the floor. It clattered and he backed up. "You would defend a man whose men assaulted me and my family?"

"I don't believe that's the case."

Benjamin saw his chance. He had an audience of people who were already at their breaking point. "What about all of you? What do you believe? Do you think we are making this up?" He turned 360 degrees. "Who do you believe. Us or them?"

Jake stepped forward trying to get people to calm down. "Listen up. People. Please. We won't get anywhere if we begin to turn on one another. Now until we can prove that Ray's guys were involved, do me a favor and back off."

"Don't listen to this fool," someone yelled pushing forward and bumping into someone else, causing them to lash out. Before they knew it an argument ensued among those in the room and it soon spread into the corridor.

Fists were thrown and before Sam could stop it, locals were on top of one another. One would pull another off only to get blindsided in the face by a fist. Sam fired two more rounds just above their heads. The group dropped, looking at him in fear.

"I swear to God, I will arrest every last one of you if I have to."

"You're not a cop anymore," Benjamin said.

"No. No I'm not, but this is not how we conduct ourselves. We're better than this!"

Benjamin stuck a finger in his face. "We are done listening to you." He turned and yelled to the others. "Anyone else done with this meeting follow me." He charged out and others followed leaving less than forty in the room. Ray returned through the same door he exited and shook his head.

"She's gone. I knew we shouldn't have trusted her. You should have let me kill her when I had the chance." Ray called out to his men. "Let's go."

"Where are you going?" Sam asked.

"Where we should have gone to begin with — Belfast. We are done here."

"That's it? What about Bennington? Harris? The military?"

"You're on your own!"

Sam tried to get him to listen but he wouldn't. It wasn't long before the rest of the crowd thinned out.

* * *

Later that evening, back at the Manor, Landon sat with a cup of herbal tea in the sunroom with Dakota and Beth. Grizzly gnawed on a bone that Rita had given him before retiring for the evening. Sara came into the room and closed the double doors behind her, she wrapped her arms tightly around her body as if she was cold and rubbed her arms. "Here," Beth said. She scooped up a throw blanket that was on the back of the sofa and handed it to her.

"Thank you, hon," she said, her eyes darting over to Dakota and Landon who were chatting. Dakota noticed and got up.

"Well I should turn in for the evening." She smiled politely as she passed by Sara. Beth crouched beside Grizzly and ruffled his hair.

"I should too, c'mon boy. You can bring it with you." As she was heading out of the room she turned to Sara. "Max not back yet?"

"Haven't seen him. Lately he has a knack of coming and going as he pleases."

She gave a nod and headed out leaving them alone. Sara wandered over and took a seat across from him. "Dakota seems nice."

"Yeah. She is. She's been through a lot. We all have."

"Beth was telling me a little about your time on the trail."

"Oh, was she," he said, a smile forming.

"Said if it wasn't for you she wouldn't have survived."

"I think she's got that the wrong way around. I owe a lot to her."

"Said you saved her life. That true?"

He stared at her then lifted up his top to show her the

scar from Billy's knife. Her mouth widened and instinctively she reached out to touch it then stopped halfway and pulled back. "I nearly died out there. It's strange what you see when you're on the brink of death. I saw Ellie."

"Ellie."

He nodded.

Sara's chin dropped.

"Look, Sara. I know we've all been through—"

"I killed someone," she blurted out, cutting him off. "So did Max. In fact he killed multiple people." Even though it was true it still felt strange to say it. She wanted to get it out there as she still hadn't told him. "I just thought you should know."

He nodded and looked out the window into the darkness. "I did my fair share of killing too," he replied glancing her way. "And I expect it won't be the last."

She closed her eyes for a second. "I thought you were dead, Landon. I would have never got involved with him had I known."

"Doesn't matter."

She frowned. "But you must have some reaction to it."

"You saw it. I left."

"But then you returned. Why?"

"Because I've been away too long. I realized a lot of things out on that trail, Sara. Things about myself, us, our kids, life." Landon shook his head. "Do you love him?" he asked.

"Jake?"

He nodded.

She shook her head. "I... No. Um." She stumbled over her words not thinking that her inability to be forthright was an admission by default.

"I get it."

"You do?" she asked, puzzled by his reply.

He nodded. "You were here alone. Well, you had Max but... it's normal to want to feel a sense of security. He probably offered that. I have to ask though... did you sleep with him?"

"No. God no."

"Would you rather he be here than me?"

"No. I think…" She started but in that moment her heart was contemplating the question. "You're Max's father and… more than that… you're my husband."

Landon took a sip of his drink. "I've changed, Sara."

"What do you mean?"

"Being away. Nearly dying multiple times, losing Ellie, living with very little and wondering if the next time I fell asleep someone would kill me — it changes a person." He set his drink down. "It's made me think about my decisions. My life. What matters. I don't want to live a lie."

"You're losing me here, Landon. What are you trying to say?"

"Us. You and I. Let's face it, before this we were one step away from getting divorced. I didn't want to admit it back then as I didn't know who I was without you but in those months away, I realized it's insane to pursue a life with someone unless you are 100 percent wanting to be with them. Now I know love isn't easy. It's hard work and I expected that getting married but I just felt that I was holding you back. Back from doing what you wanted to do, going where you wanted to go, and being with who you wanted to be with."

"That's not true."

He raised a hand. "Just bear with me." Landon leaned forward clasping his hands together. "Tell me that you didn't feel it too. A sense of feeling trapped in a relationship that had lost its spark."

"Every relationship loses its spark, Landon. It's called getting married."

"Does it? Nah, I understand that the dynamics change. The honeymoon period ends and the mundane can take over but…"

"Landon, what are you trying to say?"

He had this way of stumbling over his words, usually when he was having to come up with another reason to leave for his job, but this wasn't about his job, it was about them, and in all the years they'd been married she'd never managed to get more out of him than a grunt or a nod when it came to talking about them. Avoiding issues was what he was good at.

"I guess what I'm trying to say is—"

The door burst open and Sam entered, rifle in hand. "You all need to get your things now and come with me."

"What? Why?"

"I'll explain on the way but we don't have time. I need to get Carl and…"

Sara hurried over to him and grabbed him. "Sam. What is going on?"

"It's Bennington. He's back and he's not alone."

Chapter 13

Sam was frantic and putting everyone's nerves on edge. While Landon assisted him with Carl and tried to make sense of the situation, he had Sara go and alert Dakota and Beth. Fortunately with the ruckus he made, she didn't have to go far. They were already out on the landing wanting to know what was happening.

"Grab a bag, a gun and meet us downstairs. Sara, how many horses you got?"

"Enough. But what about Jake? Where is he?" she asked. Landon shot her a look but she continued. "I just want to make sure he's safe."

Sam replied as he shouldered the door on Carl's bedroom. "He's alerting others in town and holding them at bay."

"What?" Sara asked. "Well we should go and help."

"No!" Sam yelled. "With the way the meeting went tonight, this town is too divided. Right now they will welcome Bennington back. Believe me."

"I don't get it. What are you afraid of?" Landon asked him.

"I'll explain later but right now it's important that I get Carl to safety. You want to stay, be my guest but with the militia gone it won't be long before they head this way."

Sara scooped up a Winchester rifle and began bellowing orders. It was the first time he'd seen his wife take charge of a situation. While she wasn't timid, she'd never been fond of guns.

Landon followed Sam into the room. Carl was already upright in the bed. "No need to explain. I got the cliff notes version," he said.

"Come on, buddy," Sam said scooping an arm underneath him while Landon tried to help. At that moment the doc came into the room.

"What on earth are you doing? He's in no state to be moved."

"No choice, doc. You want to tend to him, you better

come with us," Sam said. They dragged Carl out of the room wearing nothing more than underwear. Sam threw a blanket over his shoulder and told Beth who appeared in the doorway to grab a bag of Carl's things. She glanced at Landon and he gave a nod.

"Landon?" Dakota said.

"Just follow."

"But what about your son?"

"Shit." It just dawned on him. "Is he not home yet?"

"Nope," Beth said. "I looked in his room only a few minutes ago."

He motioned to Dakota. "Give Sam a hand carrying him out. I'm staying here."

Sam stopped. "Landon, if you stay I can't help you."

"I'm not leaving without my son. I've already lost one kid. I won't lose another."

Sam looked like he wanted to argue but the clock was ticking and so he continued on with the help of Dakota. Beth hung back. "Go. Go with them."

"And leave you here?"

"I've got no problem with Bennington."

"No. I didn't leave you behind on the trail and I damn well won't leave you here."

"Beth. Listen to me." He looked her in the eyes. "I will be okay."

"The last time you said that, I found you in a pool of your own blood."

He smiled and put a hand around her neck and gave it a squeeze, placing his forehead against hers. "I'm not going anywhere, okay? You have my word."

She shook her head a few times until Sam called out. "Beth. You got that bag?"

"I'll be one minute."

"We need to go."

"Beth."

"Fuck." She turned and whistled for Grizzly to follow. At the top of the stairs she looked back at him. "What if you don't find him?"

"Then I will find you."

Beth turned. "Sam. Where are we heading?"

"Nautilus Island. We already have a boat that's ready."

Beth looked back at him.

"Go."

Reluctantly she went with Sam, leaving Landon alone in the house. He made his way to his son's room and took a seat on the bed, placing the rifle beside him. It had been a long time since he'd been in there. His eyes glossed over the nightstand, his guitar and posters on the walls. Under his breath he muttered, "Where are you, Max?"

* * *

Max's stomach grumbled. The smell of food was almost too much. "You'd think they'd give us one lousy piece of bread," Eddie said. "Gluttonous bastards!" he bellowed which only extracted laughter from the group gathered around the fire. One of them tossed a scrap near his feet and laughed harder.

"I swear when I get out, I'm gonna rip your head off," Eddie said.

Wood popped and crackled, and golden ash floated above the fire mixing with tendrils of smoke. Caine still hadn't returned from wherever he'd gone that afternoon. Based on Max's observations, Lindsay appeared to be his second in command while he was away. Every now and again she would look his way. In the darkness the flicker of the fire made shadows dance on her face. She really was quite attractive.

She muttered something to one of them and they tossed her an MRE bag and she got up and strolled over to him. "Hungry?"

"No shit," Eddie said. "Do you guys just get off on watching us suffer?"

She glanced at Eddie but didn't reply.

"I could eat something but I'm afraid I'm a little tied up," Max replied. She smiled and took a spoon and scooped out some of the food and brought it up to his lips. He opened his mouth and she teased him by putting it close to his lips then pulling back while making engine sounds before finally letting him have it.

Max chewed. He swallowed and closed his eyes. "Oh man, that's good. Chili?"

She nodded.

"Well that's good to know," Eddie piped up. "Now how about Eddie gets some, huh? Or are you just gonna play airplanes with him all night?"

Without looking at him she answered. "You'll get some in a minute."

He raised his eyebrows. "Great. I'll just wait here then," he said sarcastically.

A few scoops later, Max was starting to feel a little better. "Where's your great leader?" he asked.

"Caine?"

"Is there any other?"

She smirked stabbing the contents of the bag a few times and mixing it up. "Had some business to take care of."

"Right. Expecting him back tonight?"

"Maybe. Maybe not. He's been known to return the next morning."

Max nodded. "So are we expected to sleep standing up?"

"Yep," she said placing another heaped spoonful in his mouth.

He chewed a few times and swallowed. "You and him an item?"

"An item?"

"A couple."

She snorted. "No. Far from it. You could say I'm not his taste."

"Really? Too bad for him," Max said. That garnered a flirtatious smile.

"Oh please! Why don't you two just get a room? Geesh. Now can I get some food?" Eddie asked. "I'm starving here. I've seen the elderly and disabled fed quicker than this."

Lindsay turned and hollered for a guy named Bryan to feed him.

"Oh great. Just my luck. You get the hot chick and I get the guy who looks like he's straight out of *The Hills Have Eyes*." Eddie sighed shaking his head as the guy with the patch came over and began feeding him.

"So where you sleeping tonight?" Max asked.

She pointed with the spoon to a small treehouse. "Up there."

"Quite the setup you got going on here. You build that?"

"We have some skilled people among us. It certainly prevents someone slicing your throat in the night. You hear them coming long before they enter. Of course that is if they can get by our scouts."

"The guys who brought us in."

"You got it." She scraped the remains in the bag and after he downed the last spoonful she crumpled the bag and tossed it into the fire.

"By the way, the name's Max." She looked at him. "I never gave it earlier." She cocked her head and glanced at the guy beside her. "How old are you?"

"Twenty. You?" she asked.

"Eighteen."

She turned to walk back to the fire. "You got a drink? That food made me kind of thirsty."

"I bet it did," Eddie muttered. Before he could say any more Bryan shoved more food into his mouth. Max glanced at him and smiled. Lindsay returned with a canister and unscrewed the top. She pushed a strand of her hair back behind her ear as she brought up the canister to his lips. He took two big gulps and then started coughing.

Both of them laughed.

"What the hell is that?"

"I think they call it whiskey," she said before cracking up laughing.

"Lightweight," Bryan said, chuckling as he continued feeding Eddie.

Lindsay went to walk away while Max tried to keep her attention. "You never told me who you lost." He figured if he could make a connection maybe she'd cut him loose. It was worth a shot.

"I told you."

"I know — everyone. But how did it happen?"

The smile faded and he saw the pain, the same pain

that was evident in everyone who had lost a family member. Losing one was hard enough but the thought of not having anyone intrigued him. How did she cope with that?

"Maybe I'll tell you someday," she said walking away. He sighed.

"Hey come on now, don't you go cheap on me. There is still some left in that bag. You didn't scrape the sides," Eddie said as Bryan tossed the bag into the fire. "Ah man. At least can I lick the spoon?" he muttered before groaning. He looked over at Max. "The service in this place is truly horrific."

Max rolled his eyes.

"Did you honestly think that poor ass attempt to butter her up was going to work?"

"It was worth a shot."

"I keep telling you. Leave the lady loving to me. Manipulation is a fine art that takes years to master, grasshopper. Watch and learn," Eddie said scanning the females. "Hey darlin'." A girl with ginger hair looked over. "Yeah you. Come over here." The girl looked at Lindsay as if seeking her permission before she got up and ambled over. As she was making her way over Eddie muttered under his breath, "See. See. I told you. It's all in the eyes, my friend."

"Yeah?"

"Did anyone tell you…" He paused and she cocked her head.

"Tell me what?"

"Ugh. That um." He looked at Max, as if hoping for a lifeline.

Instead Max just squeezed his eyes shut, shook his head in disbelief and waited for the inevitable — which was the sound of her boots as she walked away.

"Well at least I didn't get a slap. That's an improvement," Eddie said. "I swear that pickup line was on the tip of my tongue."

Max nodded, catching the eye of Lindsay.

As the night wore on he watched as one by one the group climbed up into their Ewok style abodes and the fire began to die down to nothing more than hot, glowing cinders. He saw several of the campers fan out in different directions — the scouts, he figured. Eddie had managed by some great feat to fall asleep standing up. His head was down and he was letting out a faint snore. "Seriously?" Max said. "Eddie."

He got no answer. He was gone to the world.

Max wriggled in his restraints, feeling them bite into his skin. They itched and were too tight. He imagined by morning his fingers would be numb from having his circulation cut off. His mind began to wander, circling between his sister, his father and mother and everything that had become of Castine. Lost in thought he heard a branch crack. Instinctively he turned his head but couldn't see. "Hello?" he said. No answer.

Suddenly he felt cold steel press against his hands then his wrists, a sharp tug as if someone had tightened them, and then they went loose. "What the heck?"

"Don't say another word. And you try anything and I will raise the alarm."

He turned to find Lindsay behind the post. "Come this way."

She stuck a knife out to indicate which way to go, keeping him ahead of her at all times. "What about Eddie?"

"He'll be fine."

"Where are we going?"

"Just keep moving and stay quiet."

She directed him to a tree not far from the perimeter of the clearing. There he was told to climb up. Without hesitation he used the ladder of rope that hung from a branch higher up. When he made it to the top she was already up there. He turned and looked back. "How did you get up here so fast?"

"We have a pulley system. The foot goes in a noose, you untie a section of rope and the bags drop and up you go." He gave a nod to show he understood before looking around. A small candle in the corner of the wooden hut was providing enough illumination for him to see a bed that was made out of leaves. It was covered with blankets.

There were a few pillows, and a small table that had a few items. Across the room was a wooden closet that contained some personal belongings, mostly clothes. "Sit," she said jabbing the knife at him. He plunked himself down on the bed and squeezed it.

"Surprisingly comfortable," he said lifting his eyes.

She stood at a distance from him. "Soldiers killed them."

"What?"

"You asked how my family died. Soldiers were responsible."

"The National Guard?"

She gave a nod. "Of course they won't see it that way but that's how they died."

"What happened?"

"They wanted to confiscate weapons. My father wouldn't let them. My mother came to his aid when they shot him. She went for the gun and..." She took a deep breath. "The rest is history."

"Sorry to hear that."

She gave a nod. "What about your sister?"

"It would probably be easier to stomach if I knew soldiers had done it. At least I could blame someone. But it was a plane crash. I don't know if it was my father's fault or mechanical failure or the power outage."

"Didn't he tell you?"

"I didn't stick around to listen."

She lifted her head back and nodded. "I see."

"Yeah, anyway. I came over here with Eddie and he thought he could talk it out. Obviously the wrong choice."

"Where did you get the guns from?"

He paused for a second then answered. "From the dead. It's a long story but our group... on Castine... was attacked. The militia helped us and we managed to recover what was ours."

"They still over there?"

"As far as I know."

"And your parents?"

"There also. At the Manor Inn. My house."

She nodded and walked over to him and slipped off her jacket revealing a flimsy top that had three buttons that were already unbuttoned. There were two more below that and she began to unbutton them. His eyes dropped to her breasts and then locked on to her gaze. He swallowed hard as she forced him down onto the bed. They rolled a few times, and it would have been a lie to say he wasn't enjoying it but this was exactly what he'd hoped for — and she'd fallen for it. Knowing that she had a knife in a sheath around her leg, Max slipped his hand down and for a brief second he nearly had it until she grabbed his wrists and pushed them back behind his head, continuing to mush her lips into his.

He flipped her over and held her wrists above her head. Both of them were breathing hard and she was fully into it and that's when he knew he had to do it. Max latched on to the knife and pulled it out and brought it to her neck. "Sorry. I would love for this to continue. Believe me I would, but I don't think Caine will see it the same way you do. I gotta go." He backed up and she smiled. "Under any other circumstances. I would love to stay but maybe we can take a rain check." He backed up and looked over his shoulder then back at her until he was by the exit which was a simple rope that went down. Max stuck the blade between his teeth and slipped down the rope as fast as his body would drop. As soon as his boots landed he hurried over to Eddie and cut his ties. "Eddie. Wake up. Let's go."

"What?" he said in an almost delirious state. Right then just as they were about to leave, someone started clapping.

"Bravo. Bravo! I must say that was a brilliant performance. What do you think, Lindsay?"

She slipped down the rope. "One of the best."

Max eyed her with a narrowed gaze as Caine stepped out into the clearing along with several others who surrounded them with AR-15's. "You get what you need?" he asked not taking his eyes off the two of them.

"I did," Lindsay said staring at him.

She'd played him and he'd walked right into it.

Chapter 14

The echo of gunfire grew loud. Landon was laid back on his son's bed staring up at the ceiling, lost in thought when the staccato caught his attention. Instantly, he swung his legs off the bed and headed out of the room and made his way into the bathroom which gave him a clear shot of Battle Avenue. There, under the glow of the moon he saw several horses in full gallop turning onto Manor Drive, the driveway which led to his home. He couldn't make out who they were but they were clearly in trouble as they were returning fire. His initial thought was Sam. Had Bennington forced him back this way?

Landon bolted down the stairs almost losing his footing.

No sooner had he reached the downstairs than Jake burst through the side door, a rifle slung over his shoulder and one hand gripping the upper portion of his arm. His hand was gloved red. He stumbled into the wall smearing it with blood.

"Jake!" He hurried to his aid as more people came in: Tim Jenkins, a guy who worked for Jake, Aaron Baulman, the owner of a restaurant, and Nia Peters, a woman who worked at the Yacht Club. There were another four but he had never seen them before. Tim dropped to a knee in the doorway and unleashed a flurry of rounds. Two more hurried into the living room and took up position near the windows.

Jake groaned. "Sara. Is she here?"

"Sam took her and the others to Nautilus Island."

He smiled and nodded. "Good." He was out of breath and wincing in pain. "Bennington and a large number of military entered, shot a number of our guys. It's a massacre out there."

"Ray. Where's he?"

More gunfire ensued, a deafening chorus of bullets snapping and tearing into the home. "They left for Belfast. Bennington killed Ray's brother and from the looks of it was responsible for the attack on Benjamin and several other residents' homes to make it look like Ray was behind it. Didn't Sam tell you?"

Before he could reply a voice bellowed over a megaphone. "You're outnumbered. We've got the place surrounded. Lay down your weapons and come on out."

"Bennington," Jake said.

Landon hurried into the kitchen and pulled out a med kit. He tossed it to one of them while he went to an upstairs window to get a better look at the situation. Soldiers everywhere, too many to count, they darted in and out of bushes and trees, taking up position behind anything that could provide cover.

"Listen up!" Bennington bellowed. "You can either come on out or we'll come in, and you know how that ends." Someone smashed a window downstairs and opened fire on the military, the reaction was swift and deadly. Gun muzzles all over the property flashed, lighting up the night like fireflies. As the walls were peppered with rounds, Landon hit the floor and belly crawled his way toward the landing. Glass and debris rained down on him.

He went to the rear of the home but there was no way out. "Shit!"

Landon hurried downstairs. "Cease fire. Cease fire!" he bellowed.

"And do what? Let them kill us?" Aaron asked.

"Let me speak to him."

Jake reached over and grabbed Landon. "He won't listen."

"Maybe not to you." Landon yanked his arm away and hurried into the living room. He got close to where there used to be panes of glass, now there were only frames. "Bennington. It's Landon Gray. You hear me?"

He peered around the frame and could see some movement.

A crackle from a megaphone then he replied. "Landon Gray? I heard you were gone. I bet you wish you were now."

"I guess I'm just lucky that way."

That got a laugh out of him.

"Look bud, I don't know what has happened since I've been gone nor do I wish to get involved but I have no issue with you. You know that's true." Everyone in town knew Bennington or had heard of his reputation. Landon's introduction to him had been on a sleepy Sunday afternoon when he took Sara out for lunch. Like many weekends, Bennington was liquored up and in the same establishment that day. He was there celebrating a bet he'd just won on a horse race and was buying rounds for everyone — mostly to fluff his ego and give the appearance that the win had been much more than the actual four hundred bucks. According to him it was in the thousands but they soon learned from a sober friend of his that was horse shit. Either way, he'd bought Sara and him a round and struck up a conversation with him about planes. By any measure, his recollection of that day was good. He was on his best behavior, in a good mood and from what he could recall no fists were exchanged, which made a change from what he heard usually happened when Bennington frequented the bar. "I'm staying neutral through all of this."

"A little late for that, Landon. Is Sam in there?"

"Nope."

"You wouldn't be lying to me, would you?"

"I'm staring at fifty-odd soldiers, do you think I would be that stupid?"

He heard him chuckle.

"Then send on out Jake and his crew and after I have my men check the house I will leave you be."

"See, that is the problem. I can't do that."

"Then we have a problem," Bennington said.

"No. You have an opportunity to walk away and leave us be."

"See, I can't do that," Bennington replied. "Too many good people have lost their lives because of them."

"And you think shedding more blood is gonna help?"

Nothing but the sound of crickets and tree frogs.

"Surely there is a better way to move forward."

"There is, with those folks dangling at the end of a noose."

Landon cast a glance over his shoulder at Jake who raised his eyebrows. Clearly he was right. Bennington wasn't a man to be reasoned with. Since he'd arrived in Castine, he'd only caught wind of a few incidents that had occurred since he'd gone. But this kind of hatred went far deeper.

Jake chimed in. "Give it up. He won't listen."

Landon's thoughts went back to the cabin in North Carolina, the feeling of being surrounded, those final moments and what Beth did. Those were drug dealers. A different kettle of fish. Bennington was a local, a neighbor. He glanced outside. There was no way in hell they would survive an all-out battle with trained military and especially not this many.

He set his rifle down and removed his handgun.

"I'm coming out. I'm unarmed."

"What the hell are you doing?" Jake asked as Landon headed his way to exit through the side door. "You wanna die?"

"I have to try."

"He'll kill you."

"No he won't. Let me speak with him."

Jake raised a hand. "That's exactly what he wants you to do. You step outside, Landon, and it's over."

"It's already over, Jake."

Jake looked at him carefully as if he knew what he was referring to — him and Sara, his life here in Castine. "It's not over until you say it is. Now there must be a way out of here."

"Yeah, that door," he said pointing behind him. Jake turned, a momentary distraction, and in that instant, Landon stepped outside with his hands up. "I'm unarmed," he bellowed. "Don't shoot." Several bright flashlights lit him up and he squinted as he walked toward the silhouettes of horses and men. His pulse sped up. There was a good chance Jake was right but he had to believe there was some good left in Bennington. If he'd learned anything in his time in Pawling, New York, it was that change, real change often looked absurd in the eyes of many until it was accepted.

"Turn around and walk back to us."

Landon complied until he was told to get on his knees and lay face down. Quickly some soldiers moved in and restrained him. They strong-armed him over to Bennington and a soldier whose uniform made it clear that he outranked the others. "Landon Gray. I bet you wish you hadn't returned."

"Something like that. Look, Bennington we don't—"

Bennington didn't listen. With a quick jerk of the head Landon was shoved on past him. "Now the rest of you do the same!"

As he was being pushed forward Landon glanced over his shoulder at the sound of someone shouting "Fuck you!" What came next was deafening. A chorus of rounds shattered remaining windows, peppered walls and turned the once beautiful historic Manor into a bullet riddled structure. When the gunfire ceased, orders were given for soldiers to move in on the Manor. All he could do was watch as the military swarmed the Manor, a few more rounds were heard and then one of them emerged from the house and gave a thumbs-up. "Jake." Landon closed his eyes, realizing they had just wiped out every single one of them.

They kept him with a group of soldiers until Bennington emerged from the house. He made a beeline for Landon with a fierce expression of anger or disappointment. "Where did he go?" he bellowed.

"Who?"

"You know full well, who!"

"Sam?"

"No. Jake!"

Landon frowned. "He was inside when I stepped out."

"Well he's not among the dead. Now which way did he go?"

He shrugged. "I don't know."

Bennington looked at the guy beside him. "Then perhaps you know where Sam, your wife, Carl and the others went?"

Landon sucked in air. "Can't help you there."

Bennington nodded, a smile forming before it

vanished and he lashed out striking him in the face. "You want to play games? Take him away!"

* * *

Jake heard Bennington yelling at soldiers to tear the place apart. He'd heard the sound smashing, turning and destroying furniture as they searched every inch of that house for him but he wasn't in the house, he was on top of it. Minutes earlier, under the hail of gunfire he'd ascended the steps and searched frantically for a place to hide, a way out, anything to avoid capture. As the soldiers moved in on the house, he saw his opportunity and climbed out Max's window, lowered it behind him and scrambled up. He knew he couldn't make it out of the grounds as there were still too many, but hide, he could do that. Had the night not been as dark as it was, he was sure they would have spotted him. Even as he lay low against the shingles, hidden by one of the many dormers, he assumed it was only a matter of time before they found him. At least if someone stuck their head out he would get a clear shot and take a few of them down before he died. Fortunately it never happened.

The ruckus died down and he saw them leave taking Landon with them. Poor bastard. What was he thinking? Jake winced in agony from pain in his arm — they'd got a clean shot on him. It burned like hell. He remained there on the roof for at least another thirty minutes before sliding down the rough shingles and leaping to the ground.

With pain soaring through him, he staggered into the night.

* * *

On Nautilus Island, Sam had told them to not use any flashlights or candles. Although he was certain FEMA's military wouldn't head over to the island, there were no guarantees. As soon as the last of them were inside the house, Sam told them he would keep watch down at the dock just to be on the safe side. When asked why they didn't just stay on the boat out in the water, he said it was easier to stay out of sight if they docked it on the opposite side of the island, which was exactly what they did.

Worried about Landon, Beth made her way down to the dock on the north side. Sam was crouched by a tree with a pair of NV binoculars scanning the bay. He heard her approach and cast a glance over his shoulder.

"You should be in the house."

"Can't relax." She stood there looking out, hoping to see a boat with Landon and Max in it. "How did you know the island was empty?" she asked.

"Max. The militia were using it for a while."

She nodded. "This Bennington guy. How dangerous is he?"

"Dangerous enough."

"You think he'd harm Landon?"

"I wouldn't put it past him. The guy is a first-class lunatic." Sam ran a hand over his tired eyes and pawed at them.

"And the militia?"

"Gone."

Sam looked at her. "What made you come all the way from North Carolina with Landon?"

"It's a long story," she replied.

"You think he can handle himself?"

"Possibly."

"You don't sound very convinced."

She smiled and then it faded.

"You any good with that bow?"

"Not bad."

He was about to ask another question when he spotted something. "We got movement. Go tell the others to be prepared to leave."

"Is it Bennington?"

He shook his head. "Not sure."

Beth turned and hurried up to the house to alert everyone. With only a few backpacks they didn't have anything or anyone besides Carl that would slow them down. They gathered outside in the pool area while Beth raced back to the dock to get an update. As she came around the bend that led to the dock she saw Sam helping someone out of a boat. Her heart sank as her mind immediately went to Landon. It wasn't him.

As the stranger lifted his head she saw it was Jake.

She looked beyond him hoping to see Landon but the small fishing boat was empty.

Wrapping an arm around Jake's waist, she aided Sam in taking him into the house. As soon as they were in the door, Sara rushed over. "Jake!"

They sat him down in a chair, someone came over with water. He was panting hard and sweating as he downed the contents of the canister.

"What happened?" Sam asked.

"Bennington. There were too many of them. We couldn't hold them off. The rest of them are dead." They looked on, jaws agape. "I was lucky to make it out of the Manor alive."

"The Manor?" Beth asked. "You were there?"

He nodded.

"What about Landon?"

His head dropped and for a second, Beth thought he was dead. "Bennington took him in."

Sara took a few steps back and looked at Beth. She

could see the worry spreading. "And Max. Did he return?"

"I never saw him," Jake said. "But Landon's alive. At least for now."

Sam peeled back Jake's shirt to get a better look at his injury. Someone had patched it up in a hurry. The bandage was bright red and blood was trickling down his arm. "Tess, can you check the house for a med kit?"

She nodded and took off to the kitchen with Rita to see what they could find. Beth turned and headed for the door.

"Where are you going?"

"To help Landon."

He hurried over and slammed the door shut before she could exit.

"Are you out of your mind? There is an entire army over there."

"I'm not leaving him behind. You heard what Jake said. He's alive. That could change at any moment."

Jake spoke up. "Sam's right. You can't go over there.

You could jeopardize everything."

"Everything?" She narrowed her eyes and shook her head. "Step out of the way."

"I can't do that, Beth," Sam said. "You're just a kid."

"You can't hold me here."

"For now I can. We just got here."

"You expect me to do nothing?"

Jake backed Sam up. "He chose to stay."

"Because of Max."

"Yeah, well…" Jake said. "He wouldn't listen to me."

"Get out of the way."

"No," Sam said, his outstretched hand preventing her from getting near the door. "It's not just him we have to think about. It's all of us. We will help but I need time to think."

"Yeah, well he might not have time."

As quick as a flash she unslung her bow and brought it up, pulling back the string with an arrow in one smooth motion. "Open it. I won't ask again."

"Beth, honey," Sara said. "Lower it."

Beth didn't take her eyes off Sam for even a second.

"Open the fucking door!" Beth said loudly and with conviction.

Sam reached for the handle and pulled it back. Beth kept him in her sight as she backed out. "Look after Grizzly for me," she said before turning and disappearing into the darkness.

Chapter 15

Bennington felt vindicated as he took his first sip of hot coffee and stood at the bow of the TS *State of Maine*. He glanced out across the pier of Castine with Colonel Lukeman at his side. The chilly morning wind nipped at his ears but couldn't distract him from celebrating the previous night's victory. He couldn't wait to see that sniveling FEMA rep David Harris and rub it in his face.

Everyone doubted him.

But he was made for this. Sam Daniels, the militia, those who thought they could stand toe to toe would need to be a hell of a lot smarter if they thought they could outwit him. He breathed in the salty air as choppy waves lapped against the vessel, and twenty men on the dock kept an eye out for trouble. This time around he would do it right. There would be no ambush, no one to pull the wool over his eyes.

"Must feel good," Lukeman said holding his cup at

chest level.

"That it does, Lukeman. Finally, back at the helm where I'm meant to be." He shot him a sideways glance. "I told you. Stick with me and you won't be eating scraps from the table."

"Let's hope not."

"You still doubt me?"

Lukeman chuckled. "Don't you think it was a little too easy?"

"I told you. The war that you are waging won't be won with this," he said pulling his handgun from the holster. "This is nothing but a tool, a means of completing what you have already done here," he said tapping the side of his temple with the barrel. "You've got to know how to break these people down mentally."

"And you think that's what you did?"

"I don't think. I know," he muttered looking out again. It seemed almost too good to be true. How many years had he walked these streets, taking crap from the law, enduring the sneers and chuckles of self-righteous residents who thought their shit didn't stink? Now who was laughing?

"I think you underestimate the militia."

"Do I?" he said. "Or do you mean, you did?"

Lukeman looked as if he wasn't impressed but he was.

Bennington returned to surveying the town with admiration. This was all him. His work. His doing. Sure the manpower of the military had been helpful but had it not been for him, they would still be butting up against the unmoving force of Maine Militia. He took a few more sips then tossed the last dregs of coffee over the side of the vessel. "Understand this, colonel. I may not have your military training or experience of war but I know how these people think. Multiple times I was arrested and every time I found loopholes in the law. You see, you always have to be one step ahead. I haven't forgotten about the militia. Once I find out where they went, you can have your fun but my focus is on the people of this town."

He patted the colonel on the shoulder in a manner

that made him seem small, an insignificant part of his overall plan. "Castine is just the tip but it's very significant. Once word spreads of what we achieved, other towns opposing FEMA will either follow suit or buckle. Then I think you'll come around to my way of thinking."

Bennington went to walk away and the colonel asked, "Which is?"

"What I already discussed with you. The future. It's not in FEMA camps, or in trying to revive a dead government but in creating a new one, a new way of thinking where we sit at the table and decide the fate of others."

The colonel nodded. "You know how long I have served this country?"

"Too long," Bennington replied. "And what do you have to show for it? You still ask how high when these nobodies say jump. The same ones who have no blood on their hands but you do. The same ones that haven't felt the sting of war but bark their orders from their ivory towers, their command posts of luxury. No. They know nothing of the sacrifice you or your men have made. And what is your reward?" He got up close to Lukeman. "The knowledge that you have served your country. Let's face it, Lukeman, you are just a face in a uniform, another patriot who will be replaced by another. A number who they praise up on the way in but spit out on the way out. You know it's true."

"You know nothing of war."

"Do I? And yet I've achieved in days what you have failed to do in months. Tell me. Do I know nothing?"

Bennington relished his exchange with a man that few talked back to. He was used to giving orders, having people stand at attention and yet he could see that he didn't give two shits about that, and it burned him. It burned him to know that Bennington was right. Still. He needed a man like this at his side. More specifically he needed the men out there and Lukeman had already done the hard work of getting them to trust him. "It's not for a lack of skill or experience, colonel, that wars are lost but ineptitude of those behind decisions. With your tactical experience and my mind, there is no hurdle we can't overcome, but the decision on who you stand beside is up to you. Harris doesn't respect you. But me. I know a man who deserves more when I see it."

It was clear Lukeman was mulling it over.

Bennington didn't expect him to agree or fall in line immediately.

Little steps. It was all about small successes.

And as it stood they had just achieved a massive one.

"But of course I couldn't have done it without you," Bennington was quick to say. Flattery even if it was undeserved was the highest form of praise. The truth was he could have taken Castine without the military, it would have just taken longer.

Lukeman smiled as Bennington walked back into the ship and went to speak with Landon. He had a strong feeling he knew more than he was telling and he intended to get it out of him one way or another. He passed by several soldiers who looked relieved to be taking a break from the camp. Harris had more than enough soldiers, especially with the visit from Brooke, that's why the timing of this couldn't be any better. He fully planned on getting as much as he could done over the next few days while he had Harris' support.

"Enjoying yourself, guys?"

"Beats the camp."

"Don't get too comfortable."

Lukeman walked in and they immediately jumped to attention, dropping their plates of food. He felt a twinge of excitement at the thought of commanding the same attention. Small steps, small steps, he told himself as he walked out and made his way down to the lower levels of the ship.

There were two soldiers posted outside his quarters.

He gave a nod and they opened the door.

Inside Landon was laid back on a hard bed with his arms behind his head.

"Comfortable?" Bennington asked. He was taking a different approach with Landon than he had with Sam and Carl. That had been personal. His hate for them went far deeper than obstructing.

"You could use a few pillows in here but besides that, yes." Landon swung his feet to the floor. Bennington closed the door behind him and took out a protein bar from his pocket and tossed it to him.

"So. What can you tell me about the militia?"

"We on to them now?" Landon asked. He unwrapped the bar and took a huge bite.

"Well you obviously aren't going to give up the location of Sam and the others but the militia, you don't owe them anything, Landon."

"Why the interest? They're no longer here. They should be the least of your concerns."

"Because men like that don't walk away. They've killed innocent soldiers."

"Like you killed innocent residents?" He chuckled. "You're the pot calling the kettle black."

"It didn't have to come to this."

"And yet it did."

Bennington remained calm. There was no point losing

his cool. He just needed to find a leverage point. The question was, what was his? "Are you aware Max is wanted for murder? He killed two residents."

"That broke into the house. Yes."

"No. They were outsiders. I'm speaking about two of my closest friends. Good men. People with families. Kids."

Landon stopped in mid-chew and locked his gaze on him before continuing. "I'm sure he had his reasons."

"As do I. And yet you think that doesn't justify my actions. Why should your son get a free pass?"

Landon continued chewing. "Whatever happened, Bennington. Happened. But what you're doing now is only dividing this town. You know, when I was hiking the AT, Beth and I came across a town in New York, called Pawling. Now that was an example of what Castine could be if we would work together, not turn on one another. A house divided…"

"Doesn't stand," Bennington finished it for him. "I'm well aware of that. And I'm sure there are towns that are faring better than ours but that's them, not us. Different dynamics. Different people. Different views. Different crimes. There are many factors that come into play." He leaned back against the wall and put one foot up, the other out straight, then folded his arms.

Landon finished up the bar and tossed the wrapper. "When can I get some real food?"

"When I get answers."

"So you're going to starve me. Is that your plan?"

"Of course not. You speak of order, support and working together but that requires trust, Landon. If you can't trust me, and I can't trust you, how can either of us move forward? We are at a stalemate, don't you agree?"

Landon sighed. "I don't know where the militia went. Jake said something about returning. If that makes sense. Who knows."

"Returning. Very good." He went over to the door and cracked it open and asked one of the soldiers to bring down a plate of hot food, along with water. "See. It's that easy, Landon. Contrary to the opinions of people in this town, I don't agree with Harris and what FEMA is doing. Nor do I condone them taking weapons or killing residents but in order for things to change for the better, order must be established, rules must be set up and followed. Anything less and we have chaos and you can see where that has got us." He took a seat across from Landon and leaned forward feeling as though he'd got his attention. "I think you can play a very significant part in that change. Unlike the others you aren't tainted by what has happened as you've just arrived. Your voice may be exactly what this town needs. What if I gave you that opportunity?"

"You've lost me. What opportunity?"

"To be a mouthpiece. To stand beside me. Run this town. Bring about what you have seen in this..." he clicked his fingers searching for the name of the town.

"Pawling," Landon said.

He jabbed his finger at him. "Bingo! Would you like that?"

"Let me out and I'll consider it."

Bennington laughed. It then dawned on him. Maybe releasing him was the best thing he could do. Landon obviously had an unrealistic view of what this town could be. If he could get him to believe that he wanted the same thing perhaps... he turned and looked at him. "Agreed."

"What?"

"You are free to go. Of course, eat first. Can't have you going out without a full belly. But I want you to consider it, Landon. Talk with the others. Let them know that I'm not here to wage a war. I want to let bygones be bygones. Lay aside our differences and reach a common ground. Will you help me do that?" He took a deep breath. "For the good of this town."

Landon narrowed his gaze.

A soldier returned with a tray of food. Bennington got up and took it from him and handed it to Landon. He wanted him to feel as if he had his best interests at heart. "Eat up and then we will talk some more after you speak with the others."

"You expect them to listen after what you did?"

"To me no, but to you." He placed a hand on Landon's shoulder. "Have a little faith. Surely Pawling did." He flashed a sly grin and exited. "Let's rebuild, Landon. Start afresh."

* * *

Beth observed the huge number of men from the safety of a rooftop. There were too many. This wasn't the mountains of North Carolina or a few loose cannons. She stayed low. *How do I get at you?* Minutes had turned into hours. She'd spent the night moving from one location to the next formulating different ideas but coming up short.

A lack of sleep was beginning to take its toll as she lay there. At some point she even succumbed to the heaviness of her eyes and passed out. It was only the sound of men's voices that snapped her awake. She looked over the lip of the building and squinted. "Landon?" He was being escorted by soldiers. She watched as he was led down from the ship to the pier and allowed to walk away. "Impossible." Landon looked over his shoulder a few times at the soldiers. Her gaze bounced from him to the ship where others were watching.

Moving quickly she made her way down to the ground and took up a position near a vehicle. Peering through the glass on one side of a blue sedan she spotted Landon come around the corner and head her way.

She bounced up, startling him.

"Holy shit, Beth, you scared the crap out of me." He looked around. "Where are the others?"

"It's just me," she said as they broke into a jog heading south. "The others are safe over on Nautilus Island. You okay?" she asked.

"I'm fine. A little tired."

"Join the club," she muttered. "Why did they let you go?"

"To be frank I'm still trying to figure that out, though I have an idea. Look. Have you seen Max?"

"No. He never came back to the house?" she asked.

They hurried along Water Street before the road merged with Pleasant.

He shook his head. "We'll check there before you

leave."

"I leave?" She asked.

"I can't go back to the island with you. Not yet."

"But you just got out."

He cast a look over his shoulder. "I have work to do and no doubt Bennington is watching."

"Then I can't either," she muttered.

"He hasn't seen you yet."

She began to wave her arms and holler "Hey!"

Landon pushed her arms down and gave her a stern look. "What the hell are you doing?"

"What I should have done yesterday. Stayed put! I'm not leaving you again, Landon."

"You might have to. To find Max. If Bennington get his hands on him whatever hope of getting this town back will be gone. He'll use him as leverage or worse — hang him as an example to others."

"But he could have used you as leverage, right? He didn't."

"Few care about me. But a kid. A kid who has ties to

the militia?"

Beth looked perplexed. "But where would I start? He could be anywhere."

"The lighthouse, we used to have a fishing boat down there. He went with Eddie. Did he tell anyone?"

"I don't know. I could ask Sam or Rita."

"No, Beth, you can't go back there. If Bennington is up to what I think he is, he'll be watching. We can't risk jeopardizing the others."

"But if I can't find Max..."

Landon didn't have all the answers. He was flying by the seat of his pants on this one. "Just try."

"And you? What are you going to do?"

"Speak to Benjamin Willis."

"Why don't I like the sound of that?"

Landon chuckled as he placed a hand on her shoulder and they hurried toward the Manor Inn.

Chapter 16

The outlook was bleak. Sara gnawed on the side of her thumb, a nervous habit she'd picked up from her mother. She'd sat across from Jake for most of the night, and had managed to get a few hours' sleep. As daylight shone through the drapes bringing the large bedroom to life, she looked at Jake who was holding up well after the wound to his shoulder. Nearby, Grizzly was sprawled out, occasionally opening an eyelid.

Worry had been the rhythm of the night.

All she could think about was Landon, Max and Beth. Were they okay? Were they alive? She felt so incapable and stricken with fear. She winced as she bit too hard into her skin. "You'll eat through to the bone if you keep that up," Jake said.

Her eyes lifted and she allowed herself to smile.

He pawed at his eyes. "What time is it?"

"Just after eight."

He slung the bedsheets back. "I should get up."

"No, you need to stay in bed. Rest. You took a bullet to the shoulder," she said lunging forward and pressing him back. As her hair hung down over his face, they exchanged a moment and she realized and pulled back wrapping her arms around her and walking over to the window.

"You okay?" Jake asked.

She shook her head acknowledging that she wasn't. "I'm married, Jake."

She heard him sigh.

"What we shared was… good but I shouldn't have."

"You thought he was dead, Sara."

She gave a nod. "Still. He's back now and…"

"So that's it. You're just going to deny what you feel."

She groaned. "Jake. It's complicated."

"Is it? Seems pretty clear to me." He paused. "You're just scared, Sara. Scared that if you tell him the truth, you'll come off worse for it but is living in a marriage where you feel empty being truthful to yourself?"

"I didn't say I felt empty."

"You didn't say you were happy."

She groaned. "Uh, Jake. Marriage is more than just happiness. That comes and goes from day to day. The mundane eventually creeps in and then what... because it's not exciting, I should throw it all out the window? Act like I'm not in love because it doesn't excite me the way it did when I was single, young and without kids?"

He shifted his body, sat up in bed and ran a hand through his dark hair.

"It's not about throwing it out the window, it's about being honest with yourself." It pained her to admit how attracted she was to him or deny that she had feelings for him as she did. Seven months by his side had unearthed deep-seated feelings. She felt alive again but the second she let herself go there, the thought of her vows to Landon, and all the good times they'd shared, came creeping in. She shook her head and looked out the window at the choppy waves. The sky was a gun-metal, and dark brooding clouds loomed overhead making the day feel even more ominous than it actually was. A flock of herring gulls screeched and wheeled overhead.

"Honest? What does that even mean? Is it me coming up with reasons to justify leaving? Is that honesty?"

"It's a start."

She shook her head. "Right now I don't think any of it matters. What kind of life is this? My home is back in Castine, not here. My home is beside Landon and my kids."

"You're living in the past."

"And you're wanting me to envision a future that can never be."

Silence stretched before them.

"Oh stop playing the victim card. You're better than that!"

She spun around and glared.

"We don't get to choose how we feel but we can choose who to be with. The question is who? Who do you choose to be with, Sara? And why? Because if it's with Landon, then so be it. But just be honest. Honest with me, honest with him, but most importantly, honest with yourself. If you can live with that choice, then I can live with that. Hell, I've lived with it for years. I think I can continue."

The door opened and Tess stuck her head in. "Morning, sweetheart. You hungry?"

Her eyes darted between them and a look came over her as if she knew she'd interrupted something personal. "I'll be right there," Sara replied. She headed over to the door, placed her hand on the handle and without looking at him said, "I'll bring you something."

And like that she exited.

He wanted an answer but right now she couldn't give it as there was far more at stake. Down in the dining room, Sam drank coffee and sat with Tess and Rita chatting.

"Where did you get the food?"

"It was already here."

"Left over from the militia," Sam said. "They were here for a while."

She nodded and reached for a can of peaches. "Speaking of the militia. I've been thinking. Can't you go speak with them, Sam?"

"If they wanted to help they wouldn't have left."

"He just lost his brother. I think you should cut him some slack."

Tess snorted nearly spitting out her coffee. Rita handed her a napkin and stifled a smile. "Besides, he wouldn't listen. It wasn't me who got him to help last time, it was Max."

"Max?"

Sam lifted his eyes as he refilled his cup. "That's right. You have him to thank."

Sara felt a wave of guilt wash over her for coming down on him so hard. "Why didn't you tell me?"

"A little busy, I guess. I figured Max would."

She shook her head and stuck a fork into the can. "Anyway, are you going to speak to Ray?"

"No. Why would I?"

"Because his group managed to drive them out last

time."

Sam sat back in his seat and sipped his coffee. "It was different last time. There weren't as many and they weren't trained like the military now occupying Castine."

Sara threw up a hand. "Well we can't stay here."

He set his cup down. "We might have to."

"It's not that bad, I guess," Tess said. "Certainly a beautiful home."

Sara stared back at both of them. "Are you out of your mind? Castine is home. Not here."

"Look, I know you're eager to go home but we've all had to let go of the past in one way or another. Maybe it's time you did too."

"What does that mean?"

"I'm just saying, this country has changed. We need to change with it."

She put the can down and headed for the door but not before scooping up a rifle.

"Where you going?"

"To speak with Ray."

A chair screeched as Sam got up. "Hold up, Sara," he said as she exited the house and headed for the south side where the boat was docked. "You'll get yourself killed going over there."

"We'll die if we stay here. I won't have that asshole drive me out of my home. I have as much right to stay as anyone else."

"Look, just give me time to come up with a plan."

She spun around and jabbed a finger at him. "We don't have time, Sam. Landon is over there. Max is missing. And Beth has gone charging in like a bull in a china shop. Meanwhile we're sitting here playing happy families. If Ray won't listen to you, he sure as hell will listen to me."

Sam called back to the house. "Tess, get my gun."

Sara didn't wait for him. She could hear him telling her to hold up. That he would go with her. This wasn't a ploy, a means of getting him to take action, she just couldn't stand around anymore. It didn't take her long to reach the boat. After she boarded, Sam came running down the dock waving at her. "Hold up. You can't go anywhere without the keys," he said jangling them.

She put her hand out and he pulled back, closing his fingers around them.

Sara wiggled her fingers at him. "Come on, Sam, stop messing around."

"Carl is out of it, Jake is injured. I'm not having you put yourself in danger."

"Well that's very noble of you except I can handle myself."

"I never said you couldn't. But that's the reason why I need you to stay. I can't rely on Tess or Rita. If Bennington shows up here and both of us are gone, they won't stand a chance. Let me go and speak with Ray. You stay. Besides, Max could show up. I'm sure you want to be here when he does."

A hard wind blew in, waves lapped up against the boat causing it to rock. Sara gripped a line to steady herself. She got out of the boat and made her way over to him. "Don't let us down, Sam."

"You're alive because I haven't," he said passing her and hopping into the boat.

* * *

His arrival in Belfast was as expected. A large group of people, some of which were Ray's men, were there to meet him on the dock, armed and bellowing for him to identify himself before he even got close enough to moor. Once the boat was secured and they were satisfied that he wasn't a threat, he was quickly strong-armed to a restaurant a short distance away called the Lookout Bar & Grill.

Ray was seated at the bar by himself when Sam was brought in. They locked eyes in the mirror behind the bar. The stench of alcohol permeated the air. "Sam Daniels. Pull up a seat. Have a drink." He reached over the bar and grabbed another small whiskey glass and filled it up with some bourbon. Sam looked back at one of Ray's guys who had given him a shove.

"You should teach your men to treat people better."

"Oh, they're just a little irritated. Don't mind them.

Come. Sit. Drink."

Inside, it was a typical bar with tables dotted around the cramped space. Stools were on top of tables but a few were out in front of the bar. He took a seat and Ray slid the glass over, some of the liquid spilled as he'd filled it to the brim. One whiff of him and Sam could tell he'd had one too many. "No thanks."

"Refusing a drink?" He tutted then downed Sam's. "No point letting it go to waste."

"What are you doing, Ray?"

"Living. Living it up. And you? How's it going over on… what's it called?"

"Castine?"

He clicked fingers. "That's it."

"I wouldn't know, Bennington and the military drove us out."

He chuckled. "Ah," he waved his hand as if swatting a fly. "The writing was on the wall." Ray poured another drink and knocked it back.

"You not going to ask me why I'm here?" Sam asked.

Ray turned in his seat with a wild smile. "Sure. Okay. Why are you here, Sam?" he said finding the question amusing. "Actually don't tell me. I know. You want advice on dealing with Teresa. She's wiggled her way into your bed. Isn't that right?"

"You're drunk."

He raised his glass. "That I am! And it's glorious." He burst out laughing. "Seriously, smile, Sam. Drink. Be merry. For our days are numbered."

"And there was us thinking you could help. You can barely help yourself." Sam got off the stool. "Lee would be humiliated."

"Don't you dare drop my brother's name."

Sam turned, and smiled. "Ah, the old Ray is still in there. You know, Ray, you can drink yourself into a stupor but you can't hide from yourself. You want to sit here and drown in your sorrow. Go ahead. But know that we've all lost someone. We've all been affected by this blackout but back there..." He pointed in the general direction. "People were relying on you."

He scoffed. "Relying. They wanted my head. You heard them. I was to blame."

"Can't you see Bennington set you up? He set us all up and now all that effort from you, Lee, your men was for nothing." Sam chuckled and shook his head. "Do you know Max looked up to you? And now look at you. You're a sorry state of a man. Hiding behind liquor."

Ray got up and staggered over jabbing his finger into Sam's chest. "You don't know me. I don't owe you or anyone, anything!" he cried, raising his voice.

"Then you should take that uniform off and go out there and tell your guys that it's over. You've thrown in the towel. Called it quits and want to be left alone to drink yourself into an early grave. Or better still... wait for Bennington and his crew to show up and put you in the grave."

Ray gritted his teeth and swung at him. Sam leaned back and Ray shot by him, losing his balance and landing on the floor. "Man, you're a mess. Maine Militia. More like sad sacks of shit."

Ray roared, scrambled to his feet and charged at Sam trying to tackle him to the floor. But it was a pathetic attempt by someone who could hardly stand let alone fight. Sam threw him into a table and the chairs on top clattered to the floor. A few of Ray's men burst in with their rifles at the ready but Ray lifted a hand. "No. Get out!"

They stood there for a second, their gaze bouncing from Sam to Ray before they exited. Again Ray rose. This time he removed his jacket, took off his duty belt and rolled up the sleeves on his undershirt.

"That's it. Get angry," Sam said urging him on. He needed someone to push his buttons and get him to snap out of feeling sad for himself. There would be time to grieve later but this wasn't it. Ray cried out again and swung wildly, each time nearly losing his footing. Sam didn't need to lay one hand on him. His drunken forward momentum and inaccuracy kept him from striking Sam. His body crashed into another table, then another. It was only once Sam threw him over the bar and glasses shattered did he decide he'd had enough.

Sam took a seat at the bar and looked over. Ray looked up at him, his hand cut, and blood trickling from the corner of his mouth. "I think I'll have that drink now," he said pouring one. Ray looked at him and started to laugh. Sam joined him.

"You are one crazy asshole, Daniels."

"Likewise. Now shall we talk?"

Ray wiped his lip with the back of his hand and nodded. "Tell me more."

Chapter 17

Bennington relaxed on the back of a horse at the north end of the town where the roads, Shore and Castine intersected. The rays of the morning sun warmed his face as he and the colonel waited for Harris to arrive. He fished into his upper pocket and retrieved a small tin of finger length cigars and offered one to Lukeman. He declined.

He couldn't wait to see the look on Harris' face when he realized that everything was going to plan. Of course he probably told his colleague Brooke Stephens that the colonel was responsible, that's why he planned on making sure she knew the truth.

"You really think it's going to work, Bennington?" Lukeman asked as he adjusted himself on the saddle. "Because I've seen how these things can go south really quick."

"Like?"

"While out in the Middle East. Rules of engagement and whatnot."

"Well the only rules of engagement here are the ones that get results, and look around you, Lukeman… who's running the show now?"

"A little full of yourself, don't you think?"

Bennington cast him a sideways glance. "The results speak for themselves. Besides, don't worry, we have eyes on Landon as we speak. He's bound to lead us to the others or attract them back to Castine and when he does, we will be there to take the rest."

Lukeman shook his head and leaned forward on his horse. "I dunno, sounds like you are banking on too many things working in your favor," he said patting the horse. Before Bennington could reply, a plume of dust could be seen in the distance. Two military Humvees were approaching. The sun's light made him squint as he cupped a hand over his eyes.

"Heads up, colonel."

Time to watch Harris squirm.

The small convoy of vehicles made its way toward the checkpoint. The two Humvees came to a stop ten yards from the checkpoint. A soldier hopped out the passenger side and opened the door for Harris. He stepped out looking less than confident. Harris muttered something and Stephens got out, her hair blowing in the wind as she motioned to them and they both walked over.

Bennington and Lukeman dismounted.

"Ms. Stephens, this is Colonel Lukeman and our latest addition to the crew — Mick Bennington. A local of Castine, and a valuable asset to the cause."

She extended a hand and Bennington shook it.

"It's a pleasure."

"I've heard a lot of good things about you," she said.

"Well…"

Before he could tell her, Harris butted in and cut in front of him. "As you can see from the checkpoint, we have already taken back one of the towns. How many casualties, colonel?"

"Very few, sir." He puffed out his chest and

Bennington frowned. He could see where this was going. Harris and Lukeman were acting like he hadn't been responsible for the success of retaking Castine.

"Thanks to myself," Bennington said, making sure to give credit where credit was due. He shouldered past Harris to make it clear that he was in his neck of the woods now and if Harris thought he was going to be the alpha, he was mistaken. "I would love to share with you, Ms. Stephens, how I managed to achieve this." He turned to the colonel. "Of course with the military's assistance." He wasn't foolish enough to push the colonel to one side, especially since he had high hopes of using him in the future.

Harris made a final attempt at dominating the situation. He lifted his hand and waved it in front of Bennington as if he was some annoying fly. "I don't think Ms. Stephens has the time to listen but…"

"Actually I would be interested in hearing about it," she said cutting Harris off. Bennington smiled. There was nothing better than seeing that worm shrivel back into his shell. He couldn't wait for the day he could put a bullet in his head and be done with it but that would come in time. First, he had to deal with the militia, Landon and those who would try and put a wrinkle in his plans.

"Well that's good. Come, let's head back to the vessel. I'll tell you all about it and how we are planning on dealing with the remaining militia in Belfast."

She raised a brow. "You've discovered where they are?"

"Of course," he said, looking back at Harris. "We're not fools. In fact as we speak we are tightening the noose around those who have resisted."

Brooke looked back at Harris and he went red in the face. "Like I said, he's a valuable asset."

Bennington snorted. They waited for them to get back into the Humvee before leading them through a town of soldiers. While galloping toward the dock he got on the radio to find out from Sonny what the update was on Landon. The radio crackled.

"Tell me you have good news?"

"He didn't stay at home for long, sir."

"But he led you to Daniels?" Bennington asked.

"No. He is on route to Benjamin Willis' home."

"Willis?"

"Yes sir."

He frowned. Lukeman looked at him. "Problem?"

"No." He smiled back but inwardly he was confused. Why would Landon head over to see him unless of course Daniels was being hidden by Benjamin. But why would he do that? He'd got word from one of his informers that Benjamin had shown up irate at the town hall meeting. His stomach sank but he kept a poker face as he got back on the radio. He couldn't let Lukeman see weakness. The truth was he knew he was taking a risk releasing Landon but in order to bring about the change he wanted, it was going to take more than roughing up a few locals. They needed to feel like he had their backs, their best interests at heart. Once they were working together he would pull the rug out from beneath them.

"Keep a close eye on them. Update me if he goes anywhere else. And Sonny. Keep your distance. I don't want him knowing we're watching."

"You got it, boss."

* * *

Landon was going out on a limb. He saw how pissed Benjamin was with those who agreed with the presence of militia. But if they were to take back Castine they would need as much help as they could get. That began by smoothing out issues and telling him the truth of who was actually responsible for the home invasions.

He expected to find a group of armed people outside, waiting to push back any threats but instead he found Benjamin cleaning up the mess in his home. His wife, Sue, answered the door. She and Sara had been friends for years. Her involvement with the community food drop to help those less fortunate had given them something in common. "Landon. Everything okay?" she asked.

"Fine. Is Benjamin in?"

"Yeah, he's out back. Come on in." He stepped on broken glass. "Sorry about the mess. We're still trying to clean up after those thugs invaded."

He nodded but said nothing. What could he say? Besides, his home was in a similar state. Bennington and the soldiers had riddled the walls with rounds and destroyed the windows. If it wasn't summer they would be in serious trouble.

The home they lived in was modest. Benjamin worked at a restaurant in town and so he wasn't exactly rolling in money but like many who didn't have much, he and Sue were kind people. That's why his outburst at the town hall meeting caught him off guard. He was known for being peaceful, funny, a real laid-back guy with a dry sense of humor.

Landon could hear hammering in the back. "He's boarding up the windows."

He looked into the living room and felt sorry for them. Furniture was torn apart, framed photos on the floor, décor that may have held sentimental value was smashed. There was thousands of dollars' worth of damage.

"You holding up okay?" he asked. "You weren't hurt, were you?"

"I took one to the face," Sue said.

"Right."

"Benjamin. Landon is here."

He was in the kitchen holding up a plank of wood and striking a nail when they entered. A turn of the head and he could tell Benjamin wasn't pleased to see him.

"Sam send you?"

"Nope."

"I'll leave you two alone," Sue said stepping out of the modern kitchen which was now in shambles. The table looked unaffected but the granite countertop had the corners smashed, and the glass-front cupboards were all shattered.

Benjamin got down from a stepladder, set the hammer on the counter and wiped his hands with a red rag from his back pocket. He was wearing a dark shirt, and stone-washed jeans. "So? What do you want?"

"To talk."

"If it's about the militia. You can forget about it."

"No, it's not. But it is about the town."

He scoffed as he crossed the room and filled a glass with water. He didn't offer any to Landon but gulped it down then wiped his lips with the back of his hand. "You know, Landon, my wife and I have lived in this town all our lives and we used to think highly of the people who lived here until the blackout. That really showed us what people were made of. Sick. Depraved. Selfish individuals. All people care about is themselves. Their survival. Their guns. Their food. Their rights. Forget everyone else. Unless of course it benefits them." He set his glass down. "I had a bad feeling about the militia the very first day they showed up here. Nothing good comes from a group like that."

"They helped."

"Helped. Look around you. Does this look like help?"

Landon scanned the room. "They weren't responsible for this, Benjamin."

"Of course they were," he barked, tossing his rag and heading back over to the hammer. "How can you be so naïve?" It put Landon's nerves on edge. In that moment he couldn't help but think of Billy and how unstable he was. "Surely you must have seen the news or picked up a paper from time to time. Militia all across the United States are antigovernment and are only helpful to those who support their cause. If they get one sniff that someone is against them they lash out. Just as they did here." He climbed back up the steps and continued banging a nail into the wood. The noise echoed loudly. Every bang caused Landon to screw up his face as he tried to get a clear thought.

"Benjamin. Benjamin!" he hollered until he stopped banging. "I'm telling you the truth. You're angry. I get that. So am I. My home has been torn apart because of Bennington and FEMA. But if you're looking for someone to blame, it's him not Ray."

He lifted a hand. "Seriously, Landon. Listen to yourself. He's even got you to suck down the militia Kool-Aid. What you forget was I was there that night. I saw them."

"Did you? Good. Then you can point out which

soldiers did this."

"What?"

"You don't believe me, or Sam, or Ray. But what about yourself? Would you or your wife recognize who did this if you saw their face again?"

"Of course."

"No you wouldn't, Benjamin," Sue said coming into the room. She looked at Landon. "He was dragged away. It was dark. I was the only one who got a good look at the soldier who did this."

Seeing he was liable to get more sense out of Sue than her husband he walked over to her. "So if you saw him. Would you recognize him?"

"Oh without a doubt."

"Come with me."

"What?" Sue replied.

"Yeah, what are you talking about, Landon?" Ben said stepping down from the ladder.

"I want to show you the soldiers that are with Bennington. You can point out the one that was responsible."

"It's too late for that."

Landon shook his head. "My family has been driven out of Castine. The militia are gone. Sam is gone and it won't be long before you will be. Trust me on that." He began to bring them up to speed on what occurred the previous night and how he was arrested then released. "You want stability? Then we need to fight for that, not back down. Now we can't do it alone. We need everyone on board."

Ben jabbed the hammer at him. "Look. I already told you. It was Ray's crew. I'm not going with you. And I want you to leave now," Benjamin said. Landon sighed as Ben returned to his work. He walked out of the room feeling defeated. Sue led him to the door.

"Sue."

"I want to believe you but…" She looked back over her shoulder.

"Please. If I'm wrong, then I will accept that but I'm asking you as a friend of Sara. Come with me. See for yourself and then tell me."

"Benjamin won't like it."

"He doesn't have to know. I'll meet you at the far end of the road. You can tell him you're just stepping out to collect a few supplies."

Sue stared back at him and grimaced.

Landon told her he would wait ten minutes. If she didn't show, he would understand. With that said he turned and walked back down the pathway in front of their home and out the gate.

Everyone in the town was on edge.

No one knew who to trust or believe.

To think he could convince them was ridiculous.

After making it to the location, he sank down next to a large oak at the edge of the road and waited, watching the hand on his wristwatch. Ten minutes rolled by. He waited five more minutes before getting up to leave. He should have known better than to expect her to show. As he made his way back onto the road to walk home, he heard his name called. "Landon!"

Turning he found Sue hurrying up the road to meet him. She was wearing a blue windbreaker, jeans and white tennis shoes. Her hair was tied back in a bun. A smile formed.

As soon as she caught up, she took a second to get a breather by placing her hands on her knees and bending over. "You had better be right about this."

Chapter 18

The fist connected with his jaw sending him reeling back. Max landed hard, dust and grit getting in his mouth. He spat it out and gasped, his stomach roiling in pain. A circle of teens cheered like self-entitled Romans in a colosseum eager to watch two gladiators slug it out for their pleasure.

Eddie hurried over, bent down and placed a hand on his arm. "Ah man, I'm sorry."

"Hey! You can't be doing that. Finish him off!" Caine yelled before laughing and slapping one of his pals beside him. As a form of punishment for attempting to escape, Caine had the bright idea to pit Max against Eddie. The rules were simple: Whoever is left standing gets to live. At first both of them refused, telling him he was out of his mind and that he could screw himself. That act of defiance was met with brutality as Caine had three of his guys pound on Eddie until Max agreed. Caine was too smart for his own good.

On the ground, Max looked up and saw Lindsay.

He still couldn't believe she had set him up. There he was thinking she was actually interested when all she wanted was to get him to spill the beans on where more guns could be found. Now she looked as if she had second thoughts. A few times he saw her speak with Caine as if attempting to get him to stop the fight, but Caine simply waved her off and joined the others in cheering them on. Bets were placed but instead of money they were wagering cigarettes, weed and alcohol. Some small kid with a limp was in charge of it.

"If you don't finish him—"

Before he could tell Eddie what would happen to him, Max reared back his foot and smashed it into Eddie's shin then flipped over and took his other leg out from beneath him. He landed hard, air expelled from his lungs as Max scrambled over and landed on top of him. Getting close to Eddie's face while pounding his ribs with a fist, he told Eddie to play along and shove him toward Caine. "What?

No."

"Just do it, Eddie. You want out of here?"

Another sharp jab to the gut. "Ugh, do you have to hit me so hard?"

"Has to be realistic," Max said. "Now shove me off."

Eddie used his legs to flip Max over him. He landed hard a few feet from Caine. The crowd backed up to give them room. Max had already seen what he was going for, if he could just get close enough to grab it. There was only one way out of this situation and that was to cut the head off the snake, and he was more than prepared to do that now they'd come this far.

Groaning on the ground, Eddie came at him and did a soccer kick to his gut sending him rolling toward the crowd. They backed up again but with the forest surrounding them there was only so much room. The next time Eddie came at him, he caught his foot and twisted it and then dived on top of his back and started raining fists down on him then pressing his face into the dirt. "Dude, I can't breathe."

"Get up. Last time."

He couldn't speak too loudly otherwise those around them would hear.

Max got off Eddie and lifted his arm as if he had won. He purposely turned his back to Eddie and looked at Caine and waited. "I win," he announced. Caine shook his head and gave a smirk. Max knew Eddie was on his feet and any second now he would...

A hand from behind thrust him full force into Caine. Max landed on Caine shoving him back, leaving Max with Caine's knife in his hand. He swung around Caine in a flash and brought the blade up to his neck. "I will do it! Now back off!" he bellowed loudly as guns were brought up. All over the camp the sound of guns cocking could be heard. With one of Max's arms wrapped around him, the other with a knife tight against his neck, Caine couldn't get out of it, not without getting cut. Max fed into that fear by whispering in his ear. "You move an inch and you'll be smiling out your neck." He swung Caine around, using him as a human shield. "Eddie. Get his gun."

Eddie rushed in and removed his handgun. As soon as he had that in his hands he became a different person entirely. "All right you motherfuckers, who wants to be the first to taste lead?"

Max's brow furrowed. "Eddie."

Eddie glanced at him. "A little too much?"

Max pulled a face. "Just a touch." He then shifted his focus back to Caine. "Now tell them to drop their weapons."

"Do you honestly think you'll get out of here?"

"I dunno, I like the odds. Now tell them!" Max bellowed.

"Lower your guns."

"Not lower. Drop them!" Max demanded. "Over there."

All eyes were on Caine, waiting for his word. Max had a feeling if he told them to shoot they would have. It was a precarious position they were in and there was a good chance they would die but the alternative wasn't good either. All around the camp, teens dropped their rifles, handguns and anything else that could be used as a weapon. They tossed them into a pile not far from the firepit. "That's it. Now who's the bitch?" Eddie said roaming in front of them like a toothless lion, all courage but lacking bite.

Max dragged Caine backwards and had him tell the others to head east away from the camp. He wanted to put as much distance as possible between them and the weapons. There were too many guns for them to carry but they could at least take a few so this whole event wouldn't be for nothing.

Caine began chuckling. "You are so screwed."

"Really? I'm not the one with a blade to my neck, asshole!"

As the group of teens headed off into the surrounding forest, Max had Eddie tie up Caine's wrists and then they shoved a rag into his mouth to keep him quiet. Max then pushed him forward while keeping a firm grip on his arm.

"We're taking him with us?" Eddie asked.

"We leave him here we won't make it out," Max replied. "They'll return and hunt us down."

"But he'll slow us down."

Caine said something but nothing came out but a muffled noise.

"We'll take him as far as the shore then leave him. I'll lead the way, you watch my six." Eddie gathered up some of the rifles in a duffel bag he found in one of the tents and slung it over his shoulder. Next, Max and Eddie took off heading northwest back to where they'd left the boat. Trudging through the habitat of rocky trails, Eddie tried to convince Max to kill him.

"He doesn't deserve to live."

"Eddie. He's an asshole. There's no denying that but I'm not killing him."

"Then I'll do it," Eddie replied.

Caine sneered and they heard some muffled reply before Max said, "Neither are you. We're better than that."

"It's not about being better, Max, or payback, it's

about ensuring he doesn't get to do this to anyone else."

He could see Eddie's point and in a country that was now lawless, would anyone miss this kid? Probably not. Would they get arrested? Nope. But was it right? That was debatable depending on who was asked. They continued on, moving as quickly as they could. Not far from the camp they heard the sound of gunfire.

"They're coming."

Both of them picked up the pace. At one point, Caine stumbled and hit the ground. Max lifted him up but he was like a deadweight. It was as if he was doing it on purpose to slow them down. In the distance they could hear hooting and hollering. His group was getting closer. Their voices sounded as if they were trying to hedge them in on both sides.

"Move. Faster!" Eddie said. Panic crept up in Max's chest, the ever looming sense that they weren't going to make it. The terrain was also getting harder with huge boulders, steep slopes and knotty tree roots sticking out — threatening to trip them at any moment.

His throat felt on fire from running.

A second later, his boot caught on a tree root and he went head over heels. Caine saw his moment and plowed into Eddie, forcing him over a boulder, then kicked Max in the face before zipping left. He slalomed in and out of the trees as Max fired a few rounds. "Damn it!" he bellowed as he scrambled to his feet. His ankle was throbbing badly. Max limped down a slope to find Eddie injured but not unconscious.

"Sorry man, I lost my footing. Up you get," Max said scooping an arm around Eddie's and lifting him.

It wasn't long before the snap of bullets resumed in their general direction.

"Go! Go!" Max said, pushing Eddie on.

Racing through the forest they made it out to the western side of the island. Max pitched sideways down a gravel slope nearly losing his footing again. Pain surged up from his ankle. "They're gaining on us," Eddie said before unloading a few rounds behind them. As they came over a rise that should have given them a clear shot of the dock and boat, his stomach caught in his throat. "Where is it?"

"What?" Eddie asked whirling around to take a look.

"This was the spot, right?"

He nodded. The boat was gone. Nothing. They hurried down to the dock to take a closer look just in case the rope had come loose and it had drifted but it hadn't. More gunfire, this time bullets tore up the earth around them. Max darted out of view behind a boulder as did Eddie. Then, Caine yelled, "Like I said, Max. Do you honestly think you are getting out of here?"

He didn't respond.

"What now?" Eddie muttered.

"Swim."

"Swim? You know how far it is to Castine from here?"

"I'm not suggesting swimming there. We head for Nautilus. It's got to be less than a mile."

More rounds echoed, stone chipped and rained down on them.

"Come on, Max. There's nowhere to go."

Max stared at Eddie. "You ready?"

"Fuck it."

"On three."

They could hear the sound of boots. Those from the camp making their way down.

Crouched behind the boulder, out of sight, Max eyed the water. "One, two, three." Both of them blasted away and dove into the chilly waters. The slap of cold took his breath away as he disappeared into the deep. All around, rounds snapped into the water, bubbles trailing behind each one. Any second now and one would strike him. It didn't. He glanced to his right to see Eddie swimming hard through the murky waters.

They stayed beneath, kicking and pushing back the water with all their strength and only coming up when they could no longer hold their breath. By that point they were far enough out to no longer be at risk of being shot.

Max gasped and spat water like a fish. He glanced back and squinted. Under the brightness of the sun's light he saw Caine, and his group dotted throughout the steep rocky incline. A smile formed as he brought up a middle finger. Could Caine see it through binoculars? God, he hoped so.

* * *

Beth had zero luck finding Max. She'd spent the better part of the day searching Castine but had come up empty. After returning to the Manor and waiting for Landon to get back, she soon discovered she'd been followed. The sound of horses' hooves alerted her to their presence. Instead of waiting, she exited through the rear of the home, darted across the clearing into the surrounding forest and observed from afar. Crouched beneath a large oak she saw them. Soldiers appeared inside, moving through the home, weapons on the ready. Bennington had put a tail on them.

Without knowing where Benjamin Willis lived, she had no other option but to head back to Nautilus Island. Taking advantage of the momentary distraction and using the cover of Witherle Woods, she hurried to the shore where she'd left the boat and rowed over to the island.

Sara and Tess had been keeping watch on the water, and had seen her dock the boat. They greeted her, eager for news. "You made it back," Tess said as if surprised.

"Barely," she replied, walking past her.

"Landon? Did you find him?" Sara asked.

She nodded. "He's alive and well for the moment. They released him."

"Released?"

Together they strode up the narrow pathway that snaked through the woodland, passed the Cape Cod style cottage and led up to the main house. "Then where is he?"

"Speaking with Benjamin Willis."

"What? Why didn't he come with you?" Sara asked.

She didn't immediately reply but instead motioned to Tess. "You might want to keep an eye on the water. I did my best to shake them but I can't be sure." She didn't need to explain. By their expressions, they both knew who she was referring to. "Landon didn't want me to head back but things are too hot on the island right now. Too many soldiers."

Waiting in the doorway was Jake. His arm in a sling.

"Sam here?" she asked.

"He's gone to Belfast," Sara replied. "He left hours ago."

She ran a hand over her face as they lingered out front of the house. "What did Landon say?" Jake asked.

"He didn't. He just said he was going to speak with Benjamin."

Jake looked at Sara as if they were privy to something she didn't know.

"What about Max?" Sara asked. "Did you come across him while you were there?"

"No. I searched. He could be anywhere."

They all entered the house, barring Tess who opted to stay down at the dock. Inside, Beth went to get herself a drink. Her throat was parched and she was exhausted from having minimal sleep. Grizzly came bounding up and ran around her a few times before she scratched his head. No sooner had she downed an entire canister of water and set it on the counter than the back doors that led out to the pool opened and in stumbled Max and Eddie, soaking wet.

Sara shot across the room. "Max!?"

She began peppering him with questions but he was exhausted. Both of them slumped down at the kitchen table, water dripping off their clothes and pooling at their feet.

"Where have you been?"

"At the country club," Eddie said in jest. "You should have seen the friends we made. Oh. Their kindness knew no bounds."

Max chuckled, slapping him on the arm. "Holbrook Island Sanctuary."

"What were you doing there?" Beth asked.

He managed to summon a hand. "It's a long story."

Chapter 19

Benjamin was furious. For a second Landon thought he might throw a punch but instead he paced, a mass of pent-up anger, clenching his jaw and balling his fists. "He's telling the truth, Benjamin," his wife said. "I saw the guy with my own eyes."

"I told you—"

"I know what you said but I had to know," Sue continued, cutting him off.

Landon stood there quiet, gripping an AR-15. He figured the one person Ben would listen to was his wife. When Ben took a seat at what was left of a breakfast counter, Landon spoke up. "We need everyone to help. This isn't going to be easy and there is a good chance some of us won't be alive at the end of the day but if we don't push back, we will fall to whatever regime, rules and regulations FEMA wants to impose on us."

"But it's FEMA."

Landon sighed. "I'm not exactly sure it is, at least, in the way that FEMA may have operated before the blackout. These kinds of things can get away from people. I have to wonder how much of what Harris has ordered is sanctioned by FEMA and what is simply him wanting to save face."

Ben stared at him and nodded. "Are you sure, Susan?" he asked one last time before he made any decisions that could affect both of their lives.

"One hundred percent," she replied.

He nodded with his eyes closed and clasped his hands together. "There are three other families I can get on board but the rest of the community, I'm not sure about that."

Landon went over and placed a hand on his shoulder. "Whatever you can muster, I'm sure will be of great help."

"Then what?" Ben asked.

"That I'm still working on."

"Do you think you might be able to get the militia

back?"

"I don't know but at the bare minimum we as a community need to make it clear we won't stand by and be terrorized or threatened into a way of life that goes against the Constitution. I will go and speak with Ray and see if—"

"You might not have to," Sue said looking out the window. Landon walked over to see a large group heading up to the doorway. Sam and Ray were leading the way, behind them were Sara, Beth and Max. They entered through the partially open door without knocking. Landon stepped into the corridor and smiled as Beth hurried over and gave him a hug. Sara and Max smiled but looked awkward as if they weren't sure what to do. He motioned for Max to come over. He looked at Sara for a second and she nodded before he approached and hugged it out. Sam gave a casual salute.

"Landon."

"Sam. Ray."

Ben joined him and came out to apologize to Ray. "I

guess I owe you an apology. I should have known better." He extended a hand and Ray looked at it without expression. For a moment Landon thought he was going to reject him. He didn't. He grasped his hand and pulled him in and patted him on the back.

"No. I should be the one apologizing. We said we would protect you folks. We failed you there. I hope you'll see your way to forgive."

"Nothing to forgive," Ben said looking past him at the array of men and women outside. "Seems like more than before."

"It is. We rallied together those in and out of Belfast, as many as were willing to fight."

All of them headed out into the daylight and looked at the group of over eighty men and women all geared up in fatigues and armed to the teeth. "How did you manage to get on the island?" Ben asked.

"The same way Bennington did. You can't protect every inch of this land. But they have the main roads, most of the town and definitely the docks on the east side covered. This isn't all of us either. We have another ten heading around to the north end to deal with the checkpoints. No matter what, this ends today."

"So you have a plan?" Landon asked Ray.

"He doesn't but I do," Sam replied. "First I'm going to speak to him."

"Speak? No, Sam, that's a terrible idea. That's not a plan, that's suicide. You know he wants your head," Benjamin said.

Sam nodded, relaxed and seemingly without fear. "That he does. Except a man like that won't fall for how we did this last time. He'll be expecting to be ambushed. He certainly won't show his face unless I draw him out. I figure if we can take him, we stand a chance of the rest laying down their weapons."

That's when Landon piped up. "It isn't just him you have to worry about. Let's face the facts, Bennington isn't in the position he is now because of his own fortitude, he's there because of Harris. Bennington is just a puppet like the rest of the military."

"That's why this is perfect timing," Ray said. "Harris ⌐ here in Castine."

Sara chimed in. "How do you know?"

"Word travels fast. My crew has been doing surveillance on the comings and goings since we left." He looked at Sam, and Sam shook his head.

"And there was me thinking you were doing nothing except drinking yourself into a drunken stupor."

"Please. And let that asshole get away with murder? Come on. I was biding my time having my guys do some reconnaissance. A convoy of Humvees arrived earlier today. Word has it Harris isn't the only one that's here either. Some good friends of ours from one of the other counties said that some suit from out of the county who heads up another FEMA camp in Waterville arrived. It appears Harris has been asking for far more than he should have. Ten percent is the going rate elsewhere. Anyway, this suit brought with her a new group of soldiers to provide additional support."

"Support?"

"For ensuring that towns that resist are… encouraged to get with the program, if you know what I mean."

Benjamin's gaze bounced between them. "All right, I'll bite. You go strolling into his neck of the woods and draw him out. Then what? No matter how you play this I can't see this ending in anything else but bloodshed."

"I can," Landon said to the surprise of the others. "He released me requesting that I go and speak with you all and get you to see his way of thinking."

Ray chuckled. "And you believed him?"

"Of course not but it presents us with an opportunity."

Ray looked around. "His guys are probably watching us now."

"Oh they are," Beth said. "They followed me back to the Manor, so I figured they were on your tail too."

"Yeah they are. I saw them," Landon said. "Which means he knows you're here."

"And there was me thinking we were gonna pull the wool over his eyes," Sam said sarcastically.

"We don't need to," Landon replied, placing a hand on Benjamin's shoulder. "This community, or what remains of it is the key." He shared what he had in mind and Sara smiled.

"He's right."

Sam grimaced. "And if you're not?"

Ray nudged him. "Then this ends in blood."

* * *

Bennington felt like a king hosting an event for some elite members of society. He'd cracked open the best wine they could get their hands on, and had several of the guys whip up a meal. With so much going his way, he wanted to capitalize on it by rubbing shoulders with Brooke Stephens and learning about the work FEMA was doing before dropping his idea for handling the camp. The thought had come to him while waiting for Harris to show. It wasn't as much about taking control of Castine, as it was being at the helm of the FEMA camp. He was thinking far too small. After seeing the way Stephens listened to him at the checkpoint and shot down Harris' attempts at controlling the conversation, he was encouraged.

"So as I was saying. It's all about having the right person leading the cause."

"It seems so," Stephens replied.

Harris looked as if he was about to burst a blood vessel.

"I would welcome the chance to share some of the ideas that I have if you're open to that."

Stephens set her glass down and Bennington went to refill it. She placed a hand over the top. "Oh that's enough for me. Thank you, Mr. Bennington."

"Please. Call me Mick."

Right then a steel door groaned open and in walked Sonny. "Sorry to interrupt. Mick, you wanted to be updated when we had news."

"Yes. Excuse me," he said rising from the table and wiping his lips with a napkin. Harris raised a brow and Bennington gave him a smug smile. He hadn't felt this good in years. There was nothing like having people of real importance listen to him. He stepped outside and Sonny closed the door behind him.

"They're here."

Bennington waited for him to fill in the rest. When he didn't, he replied, "Care to be a little clearer?"

"The militia... and numerous other people including Sam, Jake. They gathered outside Benjamin's home."

Bennington turned and took a few steps down the corridor. "Huh. Maybe Landon did come through." He turned looking jovial. "Very good. Alert the others to be ready."

With that said he stepped back inside the room and updated the rest of them on the situation, once again eager to win the approval of Stephens.

"They're heading this way?" Harris asked.

"Um. Well." Bennington stumbled over his words.

"We should leave now," Harris said rising from the table and gesturing for Stephens to leave. Bennington lifted a hand.

"Whoa, whoa, what's the hurry?"

"The hurry?" Harris scoffed. "Do I have to remind you how this ended last time?"

"We were ambushed."

"And you may be ambushed again. Just because you think you managed to get through to this... Landon. It doesn't mean he listened to you. In fact releasing him was probably the worst mistake you could have made."

Oh, Bennington could see where this was going. Harris was trying to undermine him in front of Stephens — make him look like a fool. But that wasn't happening. He hadn't worked this hard to have a sniveling prick like him rain on his parade.

"It's under control. Last time we didn't have this many soldiers available to us." He turned to Stephens. "Please. Take your seat. You are safe here. If, and I say if because I am confident that I managed to connect with Landon. If they were attempting to ambush us, the last place you would want to be is out there on the streets."

Harris raised a finger to Stephens to indicate he wanted a moment alone with Bennington. They stepped outside. Harris whispered quietly, "I don't know what you think you are playing at but know this… I am the one calling the shots. Not you. You understand? The only reason you are here is because I allow it. The only reason you aren't in that camp as one of the others is because I allow it. Now I'm asking." He paused. "No. Actually I'm ordering you. Get out there now and deal with this matter while we leave under the protection of my men." He made a point to emphasize the word "my." He turned to walk back into the room but paused at the door with his hand on the handle. "Oh and Bennington. You ever try to make me look bad like that again in front of Stephens, or anyone, I will have your head."

He entered the room and closed the door behind him leaving Bennington seething.

* * *

Each of them had been instructed on what to do. Ray had dotted his men throughout the town to cover their asses if shit went south. Sara, Beth and Max had gone with Benjamin and Sue to rally together as many people from the community as possible. If they were to pull this off it would be nothing short of a joint effort. Landon and Sam stood outside Trinitarian Congregational Parish awaiting their arrival.

"You sure about this?" Ray asked them both.

"If I'm not then it's going to be one hell of a party," Sam replied with a smile before dropping a cigarette and crushing it below his boot.

Landon added, "If I'm not mistaken, Daniels, you seem to be enjoying this."

He smiled. "What's there not to enjoy? One way or another Bennington is going to get his ass handed to him."

They'd been waiting there for close to an hour before they saw a large group making their way down the road. It was hard to know exactly how many there were, but a rough estimate was more than thirty armed residents. Ray headed off to rendezvous with his men and get into position.

"We're taking a big risk if this doesn't work out,"

Benjamin said upon reaching them. "Not everyone wanted to help."

"Understandable," Landon said bracing himself for what was to come. "Well, let's do this."

He stepped off the curb into the midst of the people and made his way to the front. It looked like a group going to a rally as they walked down Main Street together, heading for the dock. There had to be a show of force. Each of them were there to protect one another.

It didn't take long before they were in sight of the soldiers.

Barriers had been erected to prevent anyone from attempting to rush the dock. Armed soldiers raised their weapons as if expecting trouble and Landon took a deep breath before telling the others to be ready. Out the corner of his eye he glanced up and saw some of Ray's guys moving across the tops of the buildings to get into position. They stopped at the intersection of Water and Main Streets. Benjamin had already told those gathered that at the first sign of trouble they were to break off to the left and right and use the stalled vehicles and buildings as cover. They fanned out as they moved forward as one unit.

"That's as far as you come. State your business," a soldier bellowed.

"Here to speak to Bennington," Landon said. "Tell him Daniels is ready to talk."

The soldier got on the radio but Bennington must have already got the heads-up as they spotted him making his way up Sea Street surrounded by armed guards. Their rifles were out in front, aimed at the group long before they were within earshot. Bennington was fully outfitted in a helmet, a ballistic vest and cradling an M4, his finger hovering over the trigger.

"Landon. You returned. Good news, I hope?" His narrowed gaze drifted over the mob and fell upon Sam. The animosity between the two of them was palpable. "I see you brought members of the town with you. Pete. Douglas. June." He reeled off names. He was all too familiar with them and probably knew their distaste for him. They gave a nod. He squinted and scanned the crowd. "Ray not here?"

"He's here," Landon said. Making it clear that a crosshair was already on him. It was a countermeasure, a last resort. He knew it was a big risk having Ray involved in this after what Bennington had done to his brother but he had to hope that Sam had got him to agree to play it cool.

"We're here to talk," Sam said.

"I'm glad to hear that. So then let's kick this off by having you place your weapons on the ground."

"Can't do that," Sam replied.

Bennington shifted from one foot to the next, a look of confusion spreading. "So by talk you mean — listening or negotiating? Because if you're here to listen that starts by... listening. And right now we see a group of dangerous individuals who are a threat."

"And we don't?" Sam replied.

Bennington smiled as if he was in control. "These soldiers are here for your protection."

Sam chuckled. "Ours?"

"That's right," he said with a nod of the head. "We can't just have anyone walking around with a gun, now can we?"

"You are," Sam said.

"That's because I've been given the uh... heavy responsibility of ensuring Castine plays their part."

"Plays their part?" Sam asked. "Let's talk about that, shall we. For this to move forward, things have to change, Bennington."

He nodded with a sly grin. "For sure."

"That means no more gouging the community. It's 10 percent or nothing. That's all they get."

Bennington laughed. "Hey I didn't set the percentage. I'm just here to enforce it and with it, ensure that the good folks of this town," he said motioning to the group as a whole, "are protected."

Sam shifted his weight. "That's interesting. You see we heard that FEMA has been requesting only 10 percent from other towns and the only one asking for more was

Harris. So do you want to clear that up?"

"It's simple really. Supply and demand. We are able to supply a larger amount of fish and supplies than other towns."

Sam scratched his temple. "Don't bullshit us, Bennington. How about you go and get Harris and we have this conversation with him? Oh and while you're at it, I'm sure the suit from Kennebec County would like to hear this too."

Bennington smiled and breathed in the salty air. "I would love to do that except they're not here."

"Really?" Sam replied. Bennington nodded. "They didn't arrive today in those Humvees?" he said pointing to them farther down by the dock. Bennington cast a glance over his shoulder and pulled a face.

"No, those are for us to use. Replacements for the one your son dumped in the bay," he said looking over at Landon, then at Max with a scowl. Max flipped him the bird and Bennington jabbed a finger at him as if to indicate he would deal with him later.

"Look, we already know they're here, so you might as well get them on the radio now or this conversation is over," Sam said.

"Landon."

"I'm with Sam on it. You should make it quick. There are a lot of people here who would love to squeeze a trigger and I don't think you want to get caught up in that, do you?"

Hesitation. A moment when Landon was certain that soldiers would open fire. Instead, Bennington told them to lower their rifles while he got on the radio. "Get me Harris." He looked back at Sam with disdain. A few seconds later Harris came on the line. Bennington stepped out of earshot to talk but returned a minute later.

He nodded. "Okay, they are open to adjusting the percentage... on one condition."

"Name it," Landon said, feeling hopeful.

"You hand over Max."

Sara rushed forward and got in front of him. "He's not going anywhere."

"All of this, is because of your son. We didn't arrive at this point because we opened fire. You might not like how I've handled matters but the facts are facts… your son opened fire on innocent civilians. They are dead because of him. I'm afraid there are consequences for that. So you decide. Your son, or the deal's off the table."

"No, there has to be another way," Landon said. He took a few steps forward and looked back at Max before getting close to the barrier. "Let's be reasonable here, Bennington."

He responded fast. "I am. More than you know!"

Landon waited, expecting him to change his mind. He didn't. Landon nodded, looked back at Sara who was shaking her head. He began weighing the odds. "What would happen to him?" Landon asked.

"He would be sent to the FEMA camp. From there I can't tell you."

Landon gave a nod. "Give me a moment, would you."

Bennington made a gesture. "By all means."

Landon walked over to Max, his back turned to

Bennington. He huddled around his family. "You're not seriously thinking of…?" Sara asked, her brow furrowed, before he cut her off.

"Of course not, Sara. It's taken me this long to see you again, I'll be damned if I'm losing another kid." He smiled at Max and wrapped a hand around his neck. Although he understood what Bennington was getting at, handing him over wasn't in the cards. This was a power move. Nothing more. An attempt to control them. "I love you, son."

He turned toward Bennington. "I'll agree to those terms but you take me instead of my son. Do we have a deal?"

Sara reached for his arm. "Landon. No."

Bennington chuckled. "Sacrificing yourself for your son and the community. That shit is noble. But so stupid." He paused. "Fine. Agreed. Take him instead." Two soldiers moved around the barrier to get Landon.

"Dad. No. You can't!" Max said coming to his defense. He raised his rifle at the soldiers. "Back off!"

A moment of yelling ensued, soldiers shouting for him to drop the weapon before Landon turned toward Max to get him to calm down. "It's okay, son."

"No it's not," he said. "We just got you back."

As Landon hugged his son and tried to get him to stay calm, the community began to protest. In the midst of it Sam brought up a radio to his lips. "Ray. Come in, over."

"Go ahead," Ray said as if expecting Landon to contact him.

Sam fixed his gaze on Bennington, brought up his weapon then replied, "Take the shot."

Chapter 20

Crack! Like a starting gun announcing the beginning of a race, one single shot echoed. Landon whirled around in time to see Bennington hit the ground, a dark bloody hole through one eye. His mouth widened as he threw himself in front of Sara and Max and pushed them back toward the safety of nearby stalled vehicles.

What came next was an eruption of loud gunfire from both sides.

He felt two rounds hit him in the back and his body crashed to the ground.

Sara screamed. Max returned fire over him while the crowd scattered and people on both sides were caught up in the crossfire. Bodies dropped, and rounds peppered vehicles. Dragged behind the rear of a car, Sara tore open Landon's shirt to find his ballistic vest. "I thought you…" Tears welled in her eyes.

"And risk dying?" he replied groaning as he pressed

back against the trunk of the sedan. All around residents and militia on the ground and on rooftops opened fire on the soldiers, killing many of them and forcing the rest back toward the vessel. Max scrambled over while Beth covered him, unloading arrow after arrow.

"Dad."

"I'm still here, son."

He hugged him tight. Across the way behind a van, Sam was slapping another magazine into his rifle. He shot him a look, saluted and went back to returning fire. "We need to get you two out of here."

"I'm staying," Max said.

"So am I," Sara added.

He could tell it was pointless to argue with them. All of them had felt the heat of battle in one way or another and come through it alive, this was no different. He gave a nod and once he had caught his breath, brought up his rifle and joined the fight.

The attack was swift and brutal.

Bennington's body still remained where it was, soldiers

retreated and the community pushed forward. In the distance he saw armed personnel escorting Harris and Stephens down to a Humvee. They were cowering beneath soldiers as the onslaught continued.

"Ray!" Landon yelled over his radio "Harris has reached the Humvee. Any update on your men at the checkpoint?"

"They're working on it."

"Better get them to try harder as those Humvees will be heading that way."

"I'm on it."

Another flurry of rounds unleashed causing Landon to drop to a crouch behind the barriers. The roar of Humvee engines, and the sound of bullets pinging off metal and concrete filled the air. "Sam! Cut them off!" he yelled pointing to the Humvees. He gave a nod and darted into an alley behind Castine Variety. The Humvees were heading for Water Street which would take them north up around the perimeter of the peninsula.

Landon pressed in to support the residents as Sam and

Ray vanished out of view.

* * *

Humvees weren't fast vehicles, with a top speed of 77 mph, but trying to keep up with them on foot would have been impossible. "This way!" Sam bellowed cutting through backyards, his eyes scanning for horses. Following Ray were four of his guys. It didn't take Sam long to find what he was looking for. Tied up outside a home off Green Street was one horse. Ray bellowed to his guys to head back up Water Street and support the others while Sam leapt onto the horse, and Ray untied it and got on the back. Sam dug his heels in and the mare broke into a gallop taking off up Captains Way. He figured he could zip across the green at the end of the street and come out over on Court Street. That road ran parallel to Water so there was a strong chance of cutting them off. How they would stop them was another challenge entirely but having them escape wasn't an option.

Ray got on the radio as they bounced on the horse, wind whipping their faces.

"Jenkins. You through?"

"The checkpoint is clear."

"Good work. Be on the lookout for the Humvees. Whatever happens, they are not to leave. Push stalled vehicles into place if you must but do whatever you have to do to block that road."

"Roger that!"

The horse was at a full gallop hurrying down the road. The Humvees would have to come out at Dyer Street and merge with Court before they could make it onto State Street which would take them up to the checkpoint. Far ahead of them, Sam saw the first Humvee swerve out followed by the second. There was no telling which one Harris was in. Sam veered the horse off the road just after Dyer and they crossed the field behind the Castine Historical Society. He glanced over at the Humvees as they hung a left onto State Street.

"How do you wanna do this?"

"Get me alongside it," Ray yelled.

"You got it."

The horse's hooves beat out a rhythm against the hard ground as they burst through a thicket of trees and found themselves side by side with the second Humvee. It swerved trying to knock them but Sam managed to keep out of the way.

"You need to get closer," Ray said.

"We get any closer and we're done."

Ray tapped him on the shoulder. "Get up behind it, and then veer around fast and pull away."

"You sure?"

"Just do it," he bellowed over the sound of the wind.

Sam gave it all he had, the horse moved up closer and then he darted to the left of the vehicle. One second Ray was behind him, the next he was hanging off the back of the Humvee. It swerved and Sam took the horse into the ditch and pressed on, glancing back to see Ray climb up. Up ahead he saw multiple cars filling up the road and Ray's guys pushing more into place. There was no way in hell that Humvee was getting through and yet it barreled ahead as if it was going to smash right through.

Sam looked back and saw the door open on the Humvee. One of the soldiers was trying to shoot Ray on top. Coming to his aid, he quickly brought the horse up the incline of the ditch and kicked the door crushing the guy's hand. The handgun dropped and disappeared behind the vehicle. Ray gave a nod of appreciation before pushing the door open and lobbing inside a grenade, then, without concern for his own life he launched himself off the Humvee and landed hard, rolling down into the ditch.

Seconds later, a loud pop was heard and the Humvee swerved, barreled down into the ditch and collided with multiple trees.

Sam yanked on the reins and brought the horse to a stop before dismounting and hurrying over with his rifle at the ready. Ray got up and brushed himself off. He'd obviously hurt himself in the fall as he was now limping.

Smoke was pouring out of the Humvee but no one got out.

"Harris?" Ray asked.

Carefully Sam approached and used the barrel of his gun to push one of the doors open. Inside, four soldiers were slumped over, Harris wasn't inside.

"He's not here."

They glanced down the road to see the other Humvee plow through the barricade of vehicles. It didn't get far before it came to a halt. Sam and Ray got back on the horse and hurried toward the carnage. Ray's men moved in on the vehicle, guns raised, bellowing at the occupants who were falling out coughing and spluttering. Smoke rose up from the engine. Harris, Stephens and two soldiers emerged, a third was slumped over the wheel, unconscious.

This time it was Sam who was quick to react. Taking out a Glock from his holster he made a beeline for Harris. Harris' eyes widened in horror; his hands went up. "Please. Don't shoot."

Sam climbed over vehicles to reach him. He grabbed him and put the barrel to his head. "Give me one reason why not?"

"It was Bennington. I tried to reason with him but he wouldn't listen."

Sam glanced at the woman who was bleeding from the head and under the watchful eye of Ray's men. "This true?"

"We were only authorized to take 10 percent not fifty. I wasn't aware of that," she said.

Harris tried to pass the blame. "No. No. I didn't authorize it."

"But you didn't stop it, did you?" Ray said limping over. "We would have helped had you been reasonable but 10 percent wasn't enough, was it? You had to have more. Now good people are dead because of it!" He lifted his gun but Sam put a hand up.

"No. Wait."

"For what?"

"The people of Castine should decide his fate." Sam looked at Stephens. "Let her go."

"Let her go?"

"If we kill them all we are no better than they are."

Ray stared back at him.

Stephens climbed down from a vehicle hood and brushed herself off. She wiped the blood from her forehead. Sam motioned to the horse. "Take it. The soldiers can go with you."

Stephens hesitated. Sam handed Harris over to Ray's guys and instructed them to take him back to town. He began protesting and pleading. "No. Please. C'mon! I work for the government. You can't do this! Please. We can talk about this. Brooke!" he yelled but she ignored him as she mounted the horse.

Sam walked over to her and looked up. "Don't return."

She winced in pain. "Trust me. I don't plan on it."

With that said she nudged the horse and it trotted forward with the two soldiers walking either side of it. Sam dropped his head and shoved his Glock back into the holster. He let out a heavy sigh before taking a seat on the tailgate of a stalled truck. Ray walked over and pulled out a pack of cigarettes. Sam took one and Ray lit it. "You know she might come back," Ray said as Sam blew out smoke. "No she won't."

"Bennington did."

Sam glanced at him. "She's not Bennington."

Ray squinted and looked over at Harris who was being led away in the distance by three of his guys. "They'll hang him."

Sam chuckled and nodded. "Probably."

"If I'm not mistaken, Daniels, you almost seem happy."

"I am. We've got our home back." He glanced at him and patted him on the back. Truth be told there was little to be happy about that day. For even though they had reclaimed Castine, it had come at a great cost. As he took a hard pull on his cigarette he thought back to what Bennington had said. Was it really Max's fault or was it the consequences of a country that had fallen into chaos?

There at the end of Wadsworth Cove Road they looked out over the Bagaduce River as the sun beat down, and reflected off the surface.

Epilogue

A month later

Few knew how Harris died, only that Sam told the community that he was no longer a threat. Although the townsfolk were given the choice of determining his fate, reaching an agreement wasn't easy. Eventually Ray took it upon himself to handle it, citing that Harris had been behind his brother's death even though Bennington had pulled the trigger. All that was known was Harris took his last breath twenty-four hours after the battle for Castine. Some said he was shot, others said he could be found hanging from a tree in the center of Belfast. Sam was quick to dispel those rumors as hearsay, telling Landon that Harris' final resting place was somewhere at the bottom of the bay. It seemed a fitting end to a man who rolled the dice on the lives of those who would have gladly helped had it not been for his greed. As for Teresa, she never returned. Though only a rumor shared by those who left the FEMA camp in the weeks that followed, they said Harris had killed her prior to his arrival. Whether there was any truth to that was to be seen.

All that mattered now was picking up the pieces.

Carl and Jake would eventually recover from their injuries and go on to work with Sam and the community to rebuild, farm and secure Castine. The challenge before them was great but if anyone was capable it was them. Ray stuck around for a few weeks but soon returned to Belfast, assuring them that if trouble raised its head, he'd be there for the community.

Landon and Sara stood at the end of the old wooden dock that Ellie had caught her first fish on as a warm morning breeze blew in, and a bright orange sun rose above the horizon. He wiped sweat from his brow and said a prayer under his breath.

"You know, I can still hear her laughter and see her smile," Landon said. Sara had her arm looped around his as they looked out across the water at the break of day. Max, Eddie and Beth were out fishing in a boat not far from the shore. "I miss her."

"Me too."

"I hope you know, if I could have done anything…" he trailed off and a tear welled in his eye.

"It's okay. I know," Sara replied, dropping her chin and giving his hand a squeeze.

He pawed at his eye and cast a sideways glance at her. "You and I good?"

She frowned. "Of course. What is it?"

"Well… I know I've made mistakes, Sara, and… I'm no Jake but…"

She removed her arm. "Landon."

"No, listen to me. I get it. I just want you to know that I get it. And if you ever feel trapped, know that I wouldn't stand in your way or hold any resentment."

She stared at him as if expecting him to expand but he didn't, instead she smiled. "Listen. Jake is a good person. Really good. He'll always be a close friend, well… not too close... but... he's not you. My home is with you," Sara said.

He studied her face and only looked away when the boat knocked up against the dock. "Oh c'mon!" Eddie protested. "You told us you never fished before." He tossed fishing lines onto the dock. "Mr. Gray. Beth is a hustler."

"What? I'm not!"

"Could have fooled me," Max said, agreeing with Eddie.

"I told you I hadn't fished in waters this large. But I've fished," Beth said stepping out of the boat with a grin on her face, and holding a huge trout in hand. The damn thing could have won a prize. "It's not my fault you two caught nothing."

Sara laughed.

Landon wrapped his arm around Max, and she did the same with Beth.

"Come on, let's go have breakfast."

"Um, hello! What about me? Hold up!" Eddie

bellowed, tripping up behind them as he juggled two handfuls of fishing gear, and multiple lines. A few seconds later he let out a howl. "Oh brother! I think a hook just went in my ass cheek!"

They all broke into laughter.

* * *

THANK YOU FOR READING

If you enjoyed that series, check out Rules of Survival or Days of Panic. Please take a second now to leave a review. Even a few words is really appreciated. Thanks kindly,

Jack.

About the Author

Jack Hunt is the author of horror, sci-fi and post-apocalyptic novels. He currently has over thirty books published. Jack lives on the East coast of North America. If you haven't joined Jack Hunt's Private Facebook Group you can request to join by going here. https://www.facebook.com/groups/1620726054688731/ This gives readers a way to chat with Jack, see cover reveals, and stay updated on upcoming releases. There is also his main Facebook page if you want to browse that.

www.jackhuntbooks.com

jhuntauthor@gmail.com

Made in United States
Troutdale, OR
10/05/2024

23456187R00206